BECOMING SKYE

KELSIE STELTING

For my mom - the woman who
passed her love of books on to me.

CONTENTS

LOVING SKYE: SNEAK PEEK

CHAPTER ONE

SOMETHING UNCOMFORTABLE WAS PUSHING air into my nose. Oxygen tubing. I glanced to one side of the room. Things seemed fuzzy, but I saw two chairs, one bench, and a lot of monitors. From the looks of it, I was in recovery.

Then I stared down. Blankets covered my lower half, and I pulled them back, careful not to dislodge the padded clamp on my index finger. An enormous brace covered my leg. And I realized it hurt—a slow, aching pain that began at the core of my knee and radiated out.

A hunger pang competed with the aching in my leg.

Why wasn't anyone feeding me?

I looked around for the call button, and my gaze

landed on the most beautiful pair of brown eyes I'd even seen in my life. "Kellum?"

I had to be dreaming. The best dream in the world.

He nodded and rubbed my arm through the blanket. "Hey, Skye."

"What are you doing here, cutie pie?" I winked at him.

He chuckled.

"Oh, I love your laugh. It's so Matthew McConaughey meets Zac Efron, ya know?"

He leaned forward, an adorable smile coating his lips. "Sounds like you're a little woozy from the anesthesia."

I shook my head. "Noooooo. You're a dream boat. I mean, you know I watch you every day in A&P." I slapped his arm. "Not like in a creepy way, but like in the way T-Swift likes that guy in the house across the street... I guess that was kind of stalker-y. You get it."

He laughed again, those dreamy brown eyes dancing. "I think I do."

"Why do you date Saffron? Just 'cause you think she's cute?"

His eyes drifted down to his lap.

"Oh no, I upset you. Don't worry. I'm just a little

jealous she gets in on all of *that*." I reached out and touched his muscled forearm.

A choked laugh escaped his lips. "Oh my gosh."

I laughed too. "I am pretty funny. One of my many fine qualities."

He reached up and brushed some hair out of my face, and I held his hand to my cheek. "Mmm. That's nice."

A nurse passed by my door, her Crocs squawking on the way.

"Hey," I rasped out.

The nurse backed up and poked her head in the door. "Wow, you're awake." She walked up to my bed and rested her hands on the railing beside Kellum. "We didn't expect you up for another half hour or so." She jerked her thumb at Kellum. "This your boyfriend?"

I looked at him. "Um, I wish. Isn't he hot?"

She chuckled.

"My cousin's staying in a room down the hall, and I saw Skye's name," Kellum said. "Thought I'd come in."

He came to see me? "That's so sweet."

He smiled. "Yeah, but I better get going."

I tried to keep a hold on his hand as he stood up, but our fingers broke apart.

"Fine," I huffed. "But walk out slowly so I can watch."

The nurse let out a peel of laughter. "Girl, get it."

Kellum laughed. "I'll see you at school."

Then he walked out, and I howled at him. Because he was *fine*.

CHAPTER TWO

OH MY GOSH. No. *No no no no no.*

If the aching in my leg or my hunger pains didn't kill me, embarrassment would. Had I seriously said all that to Kellum? Please let it be a dream. I had to ask that nurse to tell me it was a dream.

Dr. Pike came into the room, followed by my parents, momentarily sparing me from mental torment that had lasted more than an hour since I woke up again. How had I said that to Kellum? What were the odds of his cousin having surgery the same day and him happening to be in the room when I woke up?

"How are you?" Dr. Pike asked.

Terrified. Broken. Hurting. Mortified. "Better than I sound," I managed.

He chuckled. "You're much more lucid than I expected. The nurse said you were a little silly with your visitor."

I sighed. "Maybe if my parents would have been there..." They would have kept me from completely making a fool of myself.

Dad shrugged. "They told us it would be a while before you woke up, so we went to get something to eat."

I scowled at my leg. They couldn't wait another hour? Or even picked up some real food for me as an alternative to the baby gunk the nurses had been feeding me?

"Can she come home with us tonight?" Dad asked.

He'd been saying I shouldn't have to stay overnight, but I felt awful and really didn't want to leave. Didn't want to ever show my face around McClellan again. Dad just wanted to save money.

Dr. Pike shook his head. "Maybe if you lived in town it would be okay, but it's already late and you guys live so far away. We want to keep her overnight."

Thank you.

Dad didn't press the point, and Dr. Pike stayed

for a bit to chat with us, but he soon left my parents and me alone.

"So what did you tell that boy?" Dad asked. "The nurse said you were being a ham."

"I don't know," I replied. I could pretend it never happened, right? "My leg hurts too bad to think about it."

They were quiet, and I wanted to fill the dead space, but I had no clue where to even start. We sat in the room for a while, Dad watching the TV, Mom flipping through a magazine, and me trying to make sense of everything that had happened.

The show ended, and Dad stood up. "Let's go get Skye some food."

Mom followed him out of the room.

I thanked my lucky stars because I'd never had to pee so badly in my life and didn't want to ask Mom for help. I pushed the call button, and the same nurse from earlier entered the room within minutes.

"What can I help you with, baby girl?" she asked.

I cringed and told her about my...situation.

"Okay. Did you bring crutches?"

"No."

"Let me grab a pair for you to use tonight, then. I'll be back."

"Wait," I said. "There was one other thing."

She nodded. "What's up, honey?"

I closed my eyes. "Was there a boy in here earlier?"

"Uh huh. A cute one."

I groaned. "And did I tell you he was hot?"

She looked at me and nodded.

"And did I..." My throat constricted. "Did I... howl at him?"

She tried to keep her lips together but smiled anyway. "Girl, it happens all the time."

I groaned even louder. "I'm going to need something stronger than this pain medicine."

She waddled out of the room, chuckling. Meanwhile, I laid in the bed, embarrassed, my left leg immobilized, unable to so much as cross my legs. I felt like my eyeballs were floating.

She returned with a set of crutches and leaned them against the wall while she moved wires, cords, and equipment around so I'd have a clear shot at the bathroom. "Do you know how to walk on them?"

I shook my head. I'd never so much as sprained an ankle.

Getting to the bathroom on crutches with a giant board for a leg was an adventure to say the least, and when we got there, she said, "Here's your throne."

Yeah. Fit for a king. You know, if the king was ninety. And in a hospital. And a pervert who *howled* at his crush.

She stood beside the toilet with me and stuck her hands out for the crutches. "Usually after surgery, it isn't as easy to void urine. So just be patient, and after a little bit, it should flow pretty freely. Push the call button when you're done."

"Thanks." For telling me how to pee.

After taking care of business, I laid around and watched TV. Mom and Dad finally came back with my food, and the smell of the burger and fries drowned out literally every other thought. I stared at the grease-soaked bag and licked my lips. That was what heaven must look like.

I took the burger and savored every single bite. It was the best thing I'd tasted in my life.

When I finished, my stomach was comfortably full, but my knee started aching, the pain taking over every sense.

"It hurts so much," I whined.

"Call the nurse," Mom said.

I did, and she came in with pills. Shortly after I took them, Mom and Dad said they were leaving to the hotel.

"Wait," I said. "Do you know where my phone is?"

Mom's eyebrows furrowed. "I think..." She walked to the closet and pulled out the plastic bag I'd filled before surgery.

"Here." She dropped the bag beside me on the bed. "Need anything else?"

I shook my head. No. Not other than to reread that message Kellum sent me and figure out how on earth I needed to reply.

They left, and I stared at my phone screen, rereading Kellum's text.

Kellum: Hey, it's Kellum. Heard you were having surgery today... Good luck. I hope it goes well.

Was that a friendly "I hope it goes well" or a I-have-a-massive-secret-crush-on-you "I hope it goes well"? Honestly, it didn't matter now.

Me: ANIKA! I'm out of surgery. KELLUM WAS THERE WHEN I WOKE UP AND I TOTALLY EMBARRASSED MYSELF. It was bad. What do I say now?

I waited. And waited. And watched some show about clothing design. And waited. And didn't get a reply.

My leg hurt, my heart ached, and I needed someone to talk to. Not just about Kellum, but about everything. The reality that I had incisions on my leg, that I might not be able to play volleyball again, or go to college, hit me harder than ever.

Desperate, I connected to the hospital's wifi and went to my Facebook Messenger app. I hardly used it since I didn't have a data plan, but now it was my only option.

I found an old message thread with my sister and thumbed out a new message.

Me: Hey Liz. Just had surgery. I'm doing alright. But I could really use your advice. Can we talk?

According to the little green dot next to her name, she was online, so I waited for her to reply. Willed her to reply.

My phone made a little popping sound as her profile picture appeared next to the message. She'd seen it.

No response came from her. Not even after five minutes.

Maybe it just hadn't gone through?

Me: Liz?

The popping sound came again.

Nothing.

I threw my arm over my eyes, closed them. Hard.

My parents couldn't stick around 'til I'd woken up because they had to leave for food. Anika apparently had other things going on. My sister didn't message me back. My leg was useless.

A tear slipped down the side of my face. I wished Shelby could see me now. If nothing else, just so she'd know how thoroughly she had won. At least one of us would be happy.

I turned off my phone without messaging Kellum. If my own sister didn't even want to talk to me, why would he?

CHAPTER THREE

MY PARENTS CAME in around nine with Dr. Pike.

"Well," Dr. Pike said, "I've told your parents this already, but I have very good news for you." He held out some pictures that looked like flesh-colored vomit. "This is your damaged ACL." He pointed at one image, then another. "This is the tissue I put in. It's a nice and sturdy graft."

Next, he showed me a page that had four different pictures of white tissue on it. "Here's the good news. Your meniscus wasn't harmed at all. I believe you'll only need a five-month rehabilitation period. Volleyball starts in August, right?"

My eyes started to water. Even though I was tired and hungry and sore, I was flying. But with clipped wings—I knew how quickly an injury could take a dream away.

"Okay, let's look at the dressings," he said and pulled my blankets to the side, revealing my legs.

I had a knee-length compression sock on my right leg and a hulking black and blue immobilizing brace on the other.

He pointed to the brace. "Let's unstrap it."

I undid the Velcro on the top, and Dr. Pike started from the bottom. Soon, the brace was open, and we were looking at the bandages on my leg. A translucent sock came up to my thigh. Underneath it, colorful bruises and blood-soaked bandages covered my knee.

"It's looking good," Dr. Pike said.

To me, it just looked like a lot of blood.

"You can shower tomorrow. Just let the water run over the bandages. In two weeks, you can peel them off. Now, try to do a leg lift."

I gritted my teeth and managed to lift my leg six inches from the bed.

Dad's eyebrows rose. "Branch couldn't do that after surgery, could he?"

"You've got a strong girl," Dr. Pike said.

Right now, the last thing I felt was strong.

Dr. Pike turned back to me. "Now flex your quad."

I flexed.

"Good, now you need to do that twenty times an hour at home. Also, do twenty leg lifts an hour. We don't want to see any weak muscles when you have your check-up with me in two weeks."

CHAPTER FOUR

I STAYED home for a week after surgery. Mostly laying around and feeling tired, sad. Mom was helpful for the first couple of days—when she was home. Then she got annoyed with me and told me I shouldn't be sleeping so much... I was glad when she went back to work.

I did spend quite a bit of time while she was gone researching for my informative speech about knee injuries. I wasn't taking any chances on missing out on college after this whole ordeal. Besides, learning everything there was to know about ACL tears was kind of soothing in a morbid way.

My first day back to school, Mrs. Valor was nice enough to let me use the hour to turn everything in. Kellum was nice enough to act like I hadn't said anything. After A&P, all I had was a couple of tests to worry about—an open-book exam in Calc and one in Spanish. *El crappo.*

I bombed the Spanish test. After weights, where I just sat and watched everyone lift, I dropped my speech off with Mr. Yen, and he said he'd give it a read-through in the next couple of days. My pain medicine wore me out, and I was exhausted by lunchtime.

Rachel got my tray for me and set it toward the edge of one of the tables. I set my leg up on a chair so it was elevated, then rested a sack of ice on top before I started eating. Several people joined us at the table, including Kellum and Evan. My attempts at partici-pating in the conversation wore me out, so I just stayed quiet and listened. Some of the girls talked about basketball—they'd made it to sub-state. Just the thought of sitting on the bench with my leg propped up, pretending to be happy for them, made me want to cry.

I was the only one left at the table when the lunch bell rang. My heart started to ache in rhythm with my leg... I felt so alone.

In desperation, I looked around, hoping a teacher would walk by so I could ask them to put my tray away from me. When none of them came close, I thought about just leaving it.

Just as I was about to attempt getting up, Kellum walked to my table, looked me in the eyes. "I've got it."

He picked up my tray and walked to put it away, then came back and handed me my crutches.

Shifting my gaze down, I tried to hide my watering eyes. "Thanks."

"You're welcome." There was a smile in his voice, something deeper than kindness.

Maybe I'd given up on Kellum too quickly.

CHAPTER FIVE

I SKIPPED basketball practices after school, claiming I was too tired to stay two more hours. I was tired, but the most pain came from watching them all play and the reminder that I'd risked my college career for a sport I didn't even enjoy. And I had a never-ending list of homework—a poem to write for English, calculus problems, Spanish verbs to conjugate. Still, I went to the party several of the moms threw for sub-state Thursday evening.

I hobbled into the cafeteria, gawking at the decorations. It felt like a shrine to basketball, McClellan High, and high school dreams.

I passed by Coach Gill, and he gave me a curt nod. "Keep walking on that leg, Hoffner."

"Thanks," I said. Was that even the appropriate response?

I continued toward a table, and he walked slowly beside me. "So, I didn't know if you were planning on coming to sub-state, but we can't bring you on the bus since you'd take up a whole seat with that brace."

I wouldn't have gone anyway because I had a debate meet that day, but still. It wasn't like a couple of seniors couldn't have shared a seat or anything.

"It's better that you rest up anyway," he added. "You look exhausted."

Keep piling on, Coach. "Thanks," I said again, caught between wanting to cry and wanting to punch his stupid pink face.

I did my best to act normal during the party, but I wanted more than anything to go home and sleep for the entire weekend. Maybe the rest of the year. I settled on passing the time by taking in the decorations.

McClellan's cafeteria was really large because the elementary, middle, and high schools all used it, evidenced by the sports plaques in the trophy case and finger-painted art decorating the walls.

My eyes fell on a huge sheet of pink paper several feet off that read "100 things to be thankful for."

The younger kids must have been celebrating the hundredth day of school.

A few of the moms and players were reading the list and fawning over some of the cuter things that had been written. There was a marker tied to a piece of string and a note that said anyone could add to the list.

I watched Shelby's mom pick up the marker and write in big letters: 52. *We are so thankful for Lexy and the example she set for the team when injured.*

Lexy walked perfectly healthily to Mrs. Reynolds and gave her a hug. "Aw, that is so sweet! Thank you."

I looked down at the thick brace on my own leg, and the back of my throat and eyes burned.

Leaving my plate on the table, I got up and hobbled away on my crutches. At least I made it to the parking lot before breaking down.

"Okay, get your homework out so I can pick it up," Mrs. Grady said in English Friday. The bracelets on her wrists crackled as she made her way down the rows, picking up handwritten poems.

When she reached my desk, she whispered, "Another winner?"

None of my classmates seemed to notice what she'd said through their distracted chatter.

"I hope so." I ripped the page out and folded over the ragged edge.

She took it from me and put it on top of her stack then continued down the row, leaving the smell of her vanilla perfume behind.

I was still thinking of cookies fresh from of the oven when she made it back to her desk.

"I'm going to do something a little different today." She shuffled the stack of papers. "I'm going to pick two at random so we can get a good mix."

Cameron groaned. "What if it's bad?"

She smiled softly at him. "Good point, Cam. I'll scan it over and make sure it's appropriate."

He pulled one corner of his mouth back but didn't protest further.

"Okay." She set the pile on her desk and pulled a sheet from the middle. "A limerick." As her eyes darted over the paper, her smile grew. "'A love limerick,'" she clarified. "That's the title."

Her eyes are blue like shaving cream,
her hair is squeaky clean,
her lip gloss tastes like sweet ice cream,

and her dad's not scary as he seems.

Her cheeks are red like candied pears,
    her smile shows how much she cares,
    and don't even get me started on her derriere.

The class giggled at that one, and I looked around to see whose cheeks were getting red.

Cam. It had to be him. But I didn't know he'd started dating anyone.

I've got the perfect girl,
She sets my heart awhirl.
Just the thought of losing her,
makes me want to hurl.

The class broke out in applause, and even I cracked a grin. Not bad.

Still smiling, Mrs. Grady reached into the pile again. As her eyes slid over the page, her expression fell.

"This poem is called 'Depression,'" she said and began reading.

The sun is shining brightly

The flowers scent the air
The grass is green and growing
The sky is blue and clear

The cloud shadows the sun
The drought wilts the flower
The crowd tramples the grass
The haze stifles the sky

The sun has fully set
The flowers have long gone
The grass has been demolished
The sky has been extinguished

The sun will never rise
The flowers will never bloom
The grass will never grow
The sky will no more gleam

When she finished reading, the class of twenty-three kids stayed silent. I tried to keep my face expressionless.

Sheldon broke the silence. "That was awesome..."

Well, he could take some credit for that, I thought bitterly.

A girl in the front row nodded. "So sad, though."

Mrs. Grady sat my poem back on her stack. "What have I been talking about since the beginning of the year?"

"Grammar," one kid smarted off.

She narrowed her eyes at him. "Anyone else?"

"Respect," Abigail said quietly.

I was hoping everyone would assume it was her poem. Abi had lanky blond hair covering her pale face. I peered at her dishwater blue eyes through the curtain of hair, thinking she probably understood my poem more than anyone else in the class.

"Yes, Abi," Mrs. Grady said. "You never know what battles someone is facing."

Mrs. Grady tapped the stack of poems. "You never know who's feeling like this. It could be the person who's hiding it the best, and one thing you say to them—one kind word, one smile... Well, that could make all the difference. It could help them feel like the sun *will* rise again. Or at least make them feel less alone."

I chewed on the inside of my cheek. No matter

how well-intentioned it was, Mrs. Grady's talk was pointless. As long as there were people like Shelby and people like me for her to beat up on, high school would never change.

A kid befriending someone who would hurt their own popularity level was about as likely as Kellum asking me to prom. It wasn't going to happen. People like Kellum and Saffron had it made without even trying. No way would they throw that away for someone like me.

I saw Mrs. Grady look at me a few times throughout class, but I kept my head bowed over my notes. I didn't write the poem to get pity. I wrote it to make sense of my own feelings. To escape them.

CHAPTER SIX

THE DAY of my first debate meet, I was a bundle of nerves. I didn't have to do anything other than my speech since it was my first time, but I barely had it memorized. On the bus ride there, Mr. Yen had me sit next to him and practice.

There was so much more to debate than I'd ever realized. I didn't just have to memorize a speech. Mr. Yen had me adding inflection, making pregnant pauses, raising and lowering my tone, speaking authoritatively, and improvising when I couldn't remember the lines. The good thing was I knew my topic like Saffron knew hair product. Knee injuries were a part of my everyday reality.

At the meet, all of my teammates scattered, either to work on their pieces or catch up with friends from other schools. I used the time to pore over my paper, trying to imprint every handwritten word on my mind.

Somehow, I made it through the first round.

And then the second.

And the third.

And by some miracle, I made it to finals, earning me a congratulatory handshake from my teammate Reese who felt my "innate speaking abilities" would "serve the team well in this momentous season."

Mr. Yen gave me a pat on the back and told me good luck.

I walked down the school's hallway to the room where I'd be performing, then walked a few feet past it to stand in the corner and practice.

"Hey, Skye."

I glanced up from my well-worn speech. Andrew. The guy from Woodman who'd talked to me after I hurt my knee.

The sweet way he looked at me with his sunshine smile stole the breath from my lips. With each step he took closer to me, it got harder to breathe.

Andrew's cheeks featured a constant blush that made his eyes seem so bright. It was hard not to reflect his happiness back to him.

"How are you doing?" he asked.

"Oh, alright, I guess." I pointed to my new white brace. "Had surgery three weeks ago."

His face fell into a sympathetic look. "That stinks."

"Yeah, it was pretty rough." I folded my speech in half so he wouldn't see my meticulously hand-written words. Proof of the fact my family didn't have a printer at home. "I was flat on my back for about a week there."

Andrew's face took on an impish grin.

That didn't seem funny to me. "What?"

He laughed. "You must not have as dirty of a mind as I do."

I reached out and swatted him on the shoulder with my speech. "Don't be dumb."

He laughed again, and I fell in love with the sound. It was light, like little bubbles coming up in a glass of soda.

"I'm just kidding," he said, fighting a smile.

"Hey!" a frazzled looking woman yelled down the hall, and every student turned to look at her. "Everyone in finals who hasn't performed yet needs to get to those rooms and perform right now. We don't need to be here 'til midnight!"

"Jeez," Andrew said. "I guess that means us."

I groaned. "I guess."

He reached a hand out and placed it on my shoulder. "Good luck...with everything."

I melted under the warmth of his hand. How long had it been since someone had touched me? Let alone a guy my age. Homecoming?

"Good luck to you too," I said, giving him a last smile before turning to leave with all the other people heading to perform.

"Hey, Skye?" Andrew called.

I looked back to see him leaning against the wall with his arms folded around his binder. "Yeah?"

"Um, I was wondering—well, I wanted to ask if..." He took one hand and put it in his pocket.

"Yeah?"

"Well..." He took out his phone. "Do you think I could have your number?"

"Oh, I—"

"Are you two in finals?" The frazzled lady had found us. Up close, I noticed beads of sweat dripping from under her bangs.

"Yeah, we are," Andrew said.

"Then go." She flicked her hands at us. "Scat."

Anger rose up from the back of my throat. We weren't children or cats. She didn't need to be so rude.

She waited with her hands folded across her chest, not even giving Andrew and me a chance to say goodbye, much less exchange numbers.

Andrew nodded at me, and I made a face at him before heading a few steps down the hall and into the room to perform.

An hour later, we sat with our teams in the school's auditorium for the awards ceremony. I clapped when Andrew took second place in his event. He whooped for me when I placed sixth.

Mr. Yen wanted to leave right after the ceremony, so I didn't get another chance to talk with Andrew before Mr. Yen herded us onto the bus.

Once we all sat down, Mr. Yen said, "I'm going to run in and get the paperwork. I'll be right back," and stepped off the bus.

"Paperwork?" I asked Reese.

He slowly unwrapped the earbuds around his phone. "Our feedback from the final round. The judges leave notes for us from finals too." He nodded toward something behind me. "Looks like someone's trying to get your attention."

I spun and saw Andrew leaning out of a window of a bus parked next to ours.

My jaw fell, and my lips curved into a grin. No way.

He pointed at me, moving his finger up and down. He wanted me to open the window.

I pushed in the little gray clips and slid the glass down.

Andrew smiled, resting his arm on the window and his hand in his chin. "Hey."

A small laugh escaped my chest. So casual. "Hey."

"Congrats on sixth," he said, impressed. "Not bad for your first meet."

Blushing, I shrugged. "You know what they say. If you're not first you're last."

Behind me, Reese scoffed. "Are you seriously quoting Taladega Nights?"

I ignored him.

Andrew shook his head. "That makes two of us, then."

"I guess," I replied, loving the way he'd said "us."

The bus doors opened, and Mr. Yen stepped on. "Let's get going."

I pulled my head back in to argue, but Taylor, a senior sitting behind me, yelled, "Not yet! Skye's gotta get the guy first!"

My cheeks flamed red, and I checked to see if Andrew had heard. Judging by his grin, he had.

Mr. Yen barely concealed a smile of his own. "Fine, but wrap it up."

Now, with everyone's heads turned toward me, I looked back at Andrew. "I think I better get going."

Taylor loudly whispered, "Ask for his digits," at the same time Andrew said, "Can I have your number?"

My hands got shaky the way they always did when I was excited or nervous. Now, I was both. Not trusting my voice, I nodded.

He pulled his phone out of his pocket and held it up, thumbs poised over the screen. "Okay, I'm ready."

CHAPTER SEVEN

ANDREW and I texted the entire evening, only pausing for dinner because my parents never wanted me to be on the phone around them.

It started out simple. *Hey, how are you, do you have any pets, blah blah blah.* But then I learned more, the real stuff. That his favorite subject was history because he wanted to work in government someday. Make a difference. That he actually liked doing homework and taking tests because it was the only physical documentation that he'd actually learned something. That both of his parents were together, happily married, and he wanted to have a relationship just like theirs someday.

His texts sucked me into this happy world where effort was rewarded and people treated each other with dignity, respect. Where every text was perfectly worded, grammatically correct, and hinted at a reality where people weren't afraid to dream.

I never wanted to tell him goodnight, but I did. Around midnight.

Andrew: Wait. There was something else I wanted to tell you.

Me: Yeah?

Andrew: Did you know I've been interested in you since about freshman year?

Me: Lol yeah right.

Andrew: No I'm serious. We were at a basketball game, and I thought you were the prettiest girl there. I'm so happy we finally met.

Wow. I literally gasped. I remembered his happy smile, his face that betrayed his every emotion, and his perfect laugh. Having someone like him interested in me wasn't a problem. At all.

———

Andrew: Good morning, beautiful.

Still in bed, eyes tired from staying up late the night before, I held the phone in front of my face and grinned. Good morning texts? I could get used to that.

I texted him back and got out of bed then worked through the exercises Dr. Pike gave me to do. Leg raises, stretches, flexing my thigh, flexing my calf. And then I ran through them again for good measure. I knew there was a chance I could go to college on a debate scholarship, but I wasn't taking any risks with my ticket to a different life.

Andrew: How are you doing this morning?

I wiped sweat from my forehead and walked to the bathroom, phone in hand.

Me: Great now. How did you sleep?

Andrew: Good. :) Couldn't wait to wake up and talk to you.

My stomach did this weird swoop thing, and I set my phone down on the counter to brush my teeth. I stared at myself in the mirror with toothpaste coating my lips and grinned. Was this seriously happening to me?

I carried my phone back to my room and sent him another text.

Me: Glad I could make your morning a little better. :)

Andrew: You did. But, I better let you go. I can't text during school. Talk to you tonight? Maybe on the phone?

For the first time in a long time, I couldn't wait to go to school, just so I could hear the final bell.

I drove to school, singing along to the country love songs, and this time, they didn't sound so sad. Inside the building, I smiled at people on my way to class instead of keeping my eyes down like usual. That was, until I saw the poster surrounded by a bunch of girls.

VALENTINE'S DAY DANCE
SATURDAY, FEBRUARY 14
BRING YOUR SWEETHEART

A small crowd of freshman had stopped to take it in—ridiculous hand-painted hearts and all.

I contemplated the dance like someone might observe a spider dangling directly in front of them: with panic. Just because I'd found a new appreciation for country music didn't mean I was ready for this. I certainly couldn't ask Andrew to come without scaring him off, and there weren't exactly guys around here knocking down my door to take me, which meant I had two weeks to find someone or go solo.

I trudged the rest of the way to A&P, not ready to hear all the buzz this dance would create. Studying—that was something I could to distract myself. But for whatever reason, the function of the gall bladder wasn't keeping my attention enough not to hear people as they walked into the room.

"What are you wearing to the dance?" Saffron asked her friend.

The friend paused for a moment, pretending she wasn't sure. "I think dark skinny jeans and that pink, ruffled top."

"Shoes?" Saffron demanded, like they were planning a rescue mission instead of an outfit.

"Black satin stilettos. Short enough to dance, tall enough to do their job."

Groan.

Throughout the day, I tried to focus on school, but something about the dance must have brought up more drama than usual. In Spanish class, I overheard someone say Kylie and Trevor had gotten into a fight and broken up. Shelby had stayed home sick, so Rachel told me in the locker room after weights that Kaiser had thought about asking Shelby to the dance. No word yet on whether he would, though. Sheldon had decided he was going "stag."

Then the biggest piece of news? Cameron had asked Saffron. And she'd said yes.

CHAPTER EIGHT

MY ALARM RANG at a god-awful hour in the morning suited only to owls and vampires, of which I was neither. But I had to wake up early for the debate meet.

I rolled out of bed, somehow managed to put on matching socks and clothes, and made myself a cup of coffee before driving to the school. The sun was still hours from coming out, but the eastern sky had this beautiful cerulean hue to it, like it was hinting at the morning to come. Even though I hated being up this early, I couldn't complain about having the entire world to myself, quiet, serene.

I got on the bus and sat down. I had to practice on my own this time because Mr. Yen wanted to work with Taylor on her persuasive speech. Before pulling out my papers, I sent Andrew a quick text.

Me: Please tell me I'm not the only one awake before the sun.

Andrew: Unfortunately, you're not.

I smiled at the screen.

Me: Are you guys going to the meet at Tighler?

Andrew: No, Rowley.

My heart fell. I'd been hoping to see him today.

Andrew: Where are you going next week?

I dug through my folder and found the schedule. We had eight meets left, and I sent them all to Andrew. We didn't have any in common.

Me: Well, that stinks. :(

Andrew: Hey, we'll hang out at state. And then this summer will be awesome. I promise.

This summer? I wanted so badly for that to be true.

Me: :) So what else are you doing this weekend?

Andrew: This, and then studying, and then homework, and then getting some volunteer hours in. NHS at my school does highway cleanup once a month. What about you?

Me: Probably working with Dad. Homework. The usual.

Andrew: Fun.

Andrew: How's your knee doing?

I looked down at my legs. I'd switched from the bulky immobilizing brace to a sleeker white one which gave me more freedom. It still hurt from time to time, but I didn't take pain medicine anymore, and I could feel it slowly getting stronger.

Me: Better. Still painful. I have an appointment with my doctor next week to see how it's healing. The bruises are gross though.

I sent him a picture I'd taken of my knee with the fresh, bright pink scar and watercolor bruises.

Andrew: Ouch. That scar is going to be killer.

Me: It's not so bad. A little more painful than a tattoo, I guess.

Andrew: Well, it looked really bad when you fell in the game.

I remembered seeing him before the game started, but had no clue what happened during or after, other than him sitting with me.

Me: So you were in the gym when I hurt my knee?

Andrew: Yeah, I told my friends I wanted to run out onto the court and see if you were okay.

I laughed out loud, earning me a glare from Reese. He sat across the aisle with an eye mask pushed up and his head cushioned on a neck pillow.

"Sorry," I mouthed, then looked down at my phone.

Me: LOL sureeee

Andrew: I'm serious. Roberto was like, telling me to sit down and stay back.

If he was being honest, I was flattered.

Andrew: It was so cool to see you play though. And of course I checked the program because I didn't even have the name of the girl I'd been crushing on since like freshman year.

Andrew: I'd always told my friends how beautiful you were.

Me: Really?

My heart pounded, and my eyes stung, but I couldn't really tell why. I chalked it up to the early hour and my loneliness. No one had talked to me like this since James, and that had all ended in flames.

Footsteps sounded down the bus aisle, and I looked up to see Mr. Yen.

"You want to swap with Taylor and do a run-through?"

Even though I could have kept texting Andrew for hours, I nodded.

Mr. Yen turned and started toward the front of the bus. I took one last look at my phone.

Andrew: Of course. I saw your smile, and I was

hooked. I'm glad I finally worked up the courage to talk to you.

Me: *Me too. :)*

From the second I sat down at the front of the bus through the final round at debate, I performed with an energy I'd only ever felt playing volleyball. Mr. Yen told me to keep up the good work, the judges told me I was a great public speaker, and at the end of the day, when I told Andrew I'd placed second, he told me he couldn't wait to see how I'd do at state.

CHAPTER NINE

MOM and I sat side-by-side in a waiting room in Austin. Last time I'd been in this hospital, I'd been getting ready for one of the scariest, biggest moments of my life. Now, two weeks later, we were waiting to hear how my recovery was going—if the surgery and the work I'd put in was enough.

A nurse came to get us and led us back to a scale. I took off my shoes, put my phone and backpack on a chair, slipped out of my jacket, and stepped on.

In that cold, oblivious way only nurses can, she said my weight out loud. Fifteen pounds higher than when I'd went in for surgery.

I felt Mom's eyes burning into my back, but I didn't make eye contact. I didn't want to admit the weight gain to myself, much less her and any one of the several medical professionals in a ten-feet radius.

The nurse scribbled something in my file, took my blood pressure—high, probably from embarrassment—and led us back to an office. It wasn't the same one as last time, but it had a bench with the same cool gray pleather covering, the same crinkly tissue paper, the same couple of chairs along the wall for guests.

I sat on the bench and pulled a book from my bag, pretended to read. Mom tapped on her phone, probably texting or playing a game.

Finally, eighteen minutes later (I counted), Dr. Pike came in with a wide smile on his face. "You look a little better than last time I saw you."

I returned his smile with a weaker one of my own. "Thanks."

He nodded toward Mom. "Mrs. Hoffner. How are you doing?"

She smiled, too, and told him she was doing fine. There was way too much grinning going on. He should tell me how my recovery was going, and then we could decide whether or not the day called for all of this toothiness.

Dr. Pike led me through a series of stretches, tests, and exercises that burned my knee and sped my breathing. Finally, he patted my thigh and sat back on his rolling chair.

"I think you're doing great," he said. "This is exactly where we'd expect you to be this far out from surgery."

What does that mean? "That's good?"

He nodded. "It means you're on the right track to a full recovery. I can tell you're doing your exercises."

Mom let out a little laugh. "Well, the scale certainly can't."

Ouch. I sent her a glare, but Dr. Pike set his eyes on me.

"Weight gain is perfectly normal after a surgery like this," he said. "You still have some swelling, which doesn't help, and you're not exercising nearly as much as you used to. It just takes time. This isn't easy."

I shifted my gaze toward the floor and nodded, my vision blurring. It wasn't easy. Not even close.

Mom cleared her throat. "When can she stop wearing her brace?"

Dr. Pike swiveled his chair so he could face both of us. "I want her to wear it for at least another month. I can't tell you the number of patients I've had who have reinjured their ACL not even a month after surgery. Actually, one gentleman from up in

Oklahoma, near the panhandle, just called me the other day. Slipped on a patch of ice. His next surgery is coming up here in a week."

My heart bungee-jumped into my stomach, hanging on by my esophagus. *Reinjured?*

He must have seen my face because he nodded. "You've got to protect your knee. And that brace is a huge warning sign that says, 'Look out. I'm not okay.'"

Midway through Mrs. Valor's lesson on the intricacies of the colon (gross), a knock sounded on the door.

She paused her explanation of a prostate exam, and Mr. Yen stepped into the room.

He gave her a small wave, and she nodded at him like she knew she was coming.

"Mr. Yen wants to talk to you all for a quick second, so I'm going to step out and get some water."

They passed by each other on his way to the front of the room, and Mr. Yen took a spot in front of the giant pull-down map of the human body.

"Since you're all juniors and seniors, Mrs. Valor was nice enough to let me step in and talk to you for a minute about the ACT."

Zack groaned.

"Yep, that's the one." Mr. Yen chuckled. "The next test date is February 28th, and unless you got a thirty-six last time, I'd highly encourage you to sign up. It's only about fifty bucks, and even a few extra points could mean thousands of dollars extra in scholarships."

Yeah, but you had to have the fifty dollars first.

"Some of you seniors are closing in on some of your last chances to take the test. You juniors need to be taking it now, seriously, so you're ready when scholarship applications roll around in the fall. I know that sounds like a long ways off, but trust me, it's not. Fall—graduation—will be here before you know it."

I sincerely doubted that. High school had been dragging by at such a glacial pace I could practically feel myself getting covered in that sediment left behind by glaciers. Moraines, I thought they were called. But, of course, that wouldn't be on the ACT.

"Does anyone have any questions?"

Crickets.

"No one?" he said disbelievingly.

When that class stayed silent, he nodded. "How'd you girls do at sub-state?"

Oh no.

A few of the girls glared off in the distance, but Zack leaned forward on his elbows. "They got creamed, Mr. Yen. Like, down by twenty in the first quarter."

Mr. Yen winced.

"Uh huh." Zack nodded. "They lost by like, what?" He turned to one of the girls who was now sending her icy stare his way. "Sixty points?"

Scowling, she nodded.

Luckily for Mr. Yen, he covered his cringe quickly. "Well, I'm sorry to hear that," he said. "But that means basketball won't be a problem for this test date."

"Skye, Taylor," he added, "we have an under-classmen debate meet that weekend, so I expect you both to sign up and take the exam. Monday's the last day to sign up."

Kellum turned in his chair and looked at me. My cheeks burned under his stare, but I forced myself to meet his soft brown eyes. The corners of his lips turned up in one of the quickest smiles I'd ever seen, and he turned back to the front of the room.

When Mrs. Valor came back in, Mr. Yen stepped out, and she continued our lesson on the colon. Seconds before the bell rang, she handed out a work-sheet, and I tucked it in my bag.

Kellum stopped by my desk on his way out of the room and dropped a folded piece of paper in front of me.

I glanced up at him, and he smiled before inclining his head toward the note and leaving the room. I felt another set of eyes on me—Saffron's. Her expression hardened, but the second she caught me staring, she smoothed her furrowed brows and walked out, chin high.

Carefully, excitedly, nervously, I opened the paper.

Don't sign up for the test yet. I have an idea.

-H-O-T hot

CHAPTER TEN

I WAITED the rest of the day for Kellum to meet me in the hallway and reveal his big plan. Or maybe just ask me to the dance. But he didn't mention the note in weights—or even talk to me really. I had debate practice during lunch that day, but that didn't stop me from imagining all the ways he could ask me out in the cafeteria with the entire, albeit miniscule, student body as his witness.

He didn't burst into debate practice or come into the calculus room and ask me to help him solve a problem—being dateless for the dance—and he certainly didn't make any news in journalism by breaking in and popping any questions.

Nothing. Zip. Nada.

Not even a single explanatory text.

I started wondering if I'd even received the note at all. The only confirmation was the half sheet of paper I kept in my back pocket, occasionally running my fingertips across the spot where I knew he'd scrawled the words.

By the time I got home, I was wound as tightly as a rubber band and had no idea what to do with all my nervous energy. I wished Andrew would text me, but he hadn't. Even though my fingers itched to text Andrew first, I restrained myself. I couldn't be that girl already. We'd only known each other for like a month, actually been talking for a week and a half, and I already felt like something was missing without his texts.

I did everything I could think of to distract myself, from homework to cleaning, and even that didn't keep me from thinking of Kellum's note. Of how much I'd already come to love hearing from Andrew.

I sat my phone displaying my favorite text message from Andrew on my desk and then carefully laid out Kellum's note.

The message from Andrew read, *I'd always told them how beautiful you are.*

My stomach clenched a little—in a good way—at the words.

And then Kellum's note. *Don't sign up for the test yet. I have an idea.*

I cringed at his signature. A nod toward the way I'd humiliated myself. But he couldn't blame me—I was under anesthesia for crying out loud.

His note was coy at best, confusing, sure, but meaningless? I'd have to wait to find out. He had until Monday.

—————

When Kellum didn't talk to me the next day, I called in—well, texted in—reinforcements.

Me: SOS. Guy troubles.

I stared at my phone screen a few minutes, hoping Anika would respond. Her family kept her busy with chores on their farm, and she hung out with her friends, Brandon and Leslie, pretty regularly. But she was the closest thing to a friend I could ask for advice right now.

Anika: Not sure how much I'll help, but Leslie is here. Expert on the subject.

I laughed a little. From what I knew of Leslie, she was outgoing and bold and totally good with the opposite sex. Unlike me. Clearly.

I texted out the situation as best as I could.

Anika: OMG. KELLUM WATTS SENT YOU THAT NOTE?

Anika: PS This is Leslie.

Anika: But seriously, Kellum?!?!

Anika: OMG Anika just told me about what you did after surgery. Yikes. Lol. Looks like he's over it though.

I blushed.

Me: I'm freaking out. I mean, I'm texting this other guy, but I've crushed on Kellum forrrrevvvver.

Anika: WAIT. Other guy? Spill. (Anika wants to know.)

So I told them about Andrew as best as I could in a text message. His sweet smile and the way his words twisted my insides didn't exactly translate.

Anika: omg, he sounds perfect.

Anika: But back to Kellum.

Anika: And that note.

Anika: Could he have been any more vague?

Me: Cryptic, right?

Anika: Um. Yeah.

Me: So what should I do?? What do you think it means?

Anika: I mean, it's a total come on. The question is why the note. Why didn't he text you or just catch you between classes?

Anika: And wasn't he dating that Stacey girl?

Me: Saffron, but, I don't think they were ever really "official." And she's going to our sweetheart dance with someone else.

She sent me a text full of surprised emojis.

Me: I know right???

Anika: Okay, so it's a good thing he's doing it on the DL. That means he's not just trying to make her jealous.

I'd never thought of that, and my chest wrenched at the idea. He wasn't going to use me, was he?

Me: The dance is tomorrow... What do I do?

Anika: Make him come to you.

I sighed.

Me: So, just... wait?

Anika: Yup. Not much else to do.

CHAPTER ELEVEN

"WHERE ARE YOU GOING?" Mom asked.

I looked down at my best pair of skinny jeans and the blue top I hoped would bring out my eyes. She and Dad were parked in their usual post-work positions in front of the television: Mom on the couch with a glass of wine, Dad on the recliner holding a tall plastic cup filled to the brim with one third whiskey and two thirds generic brand Coke.

"The Valentine's Day dance," I said.

Dad kept his eyes glued on the television. "Did you ask permission?"

I knew what that meant. He might not let me go, just to prove a point that they could do whatever they wanted, and I was stuck.

Unspoken words burned my throat and made my

hands shake. They had to let me go. "I didn't think I had to ask for school stuff."

"So you just thought you'd walk out of the house without saying anything," he said.

Preferably, honestly. "Well, it's on the school mailer."

I didn't mention that all the notes the school mailed to our house each month about upcoming events usually wound up coffee-stained and in the trash. Or that Mom had refused to take me shopping for a new shirt to wear only a few days prior.

Mom folded her arms across her chest. "And you decided to use *our* gas and drive all the way to the school?"

I looked toward the ceiling, biting back arguments. They'd saved more than enough already by keeping me at home and setting ridiculous curfews. "I thought when I asked you about a new shirt and you said I could wear an old one that meant I could go."

Mom rolled her eyes. "We're not stupid, Skye."

"I did! I've just been having a hard time with my knee, and school, and—"

Dad got out of his chair—his glass was empty. "Quit milking that damn injury,"

Ouch. I'd hardly talked to them about it—especially after how Mom'd reacted to my weight gain, but it was true. Every step I took reminded me of all I'd lost. Every exercise reminded me of how far I had to go.

Now, more than ever, I just wanted to go to the dance and pretend for a night that I was a normal high schooler with normal parents, a normal curfew, and normal friends. Any friends. And time was running out to find out what Kellum's note meant before I'd have to sign up for the ACT in McClellan.

"I'm sorry, okay? I should have asked you permission first."

Dad tipped the whiskey bottle over his cup. "You just come home, hole up in your room, don't say two words to us, and think you can make the rules."

I usually made it a rule not to apologize—especially not to my parents—unless I actually thought I'd done something wrong, but desperate times called for desperate measures. "I'm sorry."

"It better not happen again," Dad said.

"It won't," I said. "Can I please go?"

"Fine," he grunted.

"Be home by 10:30," Mom added.

"The dance doesn't even get over until eleven!" I protested. "I'd have to leave at 10:15 to get home on time."

"Then you better leave at 10:15," she said.

"But—"

"Quit arguing," Dad snapped, his face red. "You're lucky we're letting you go at all."

And they wondered why I only ever went to my room, avoided them?

I walked out the door without saying another word. I knew they'd think it was disrespectful, but it was that or scream. I'd never done anything to deserve this. Other kids snuck out, drank, and got bad grades, but they still got treated like human beings with actual brains and feelings.

Seething, I stormed down the dark sidewalk to my pickup. I hopped in and threw it into reverse.

Country music spilled out the old speakers, and I turned it up, imagining the singer had written the love song for me. I wanted so badly to have someone like that in my life. Someone who would love me. Who'd think I was precious. Who'd be afraid of losing me.

I came to a stop in the school's parking lot, but I wasn't ready to go in. Not yet.

I sat in my pickup, watching couples walk into the dance arm-in-arm, hand-in-hand.

Without the country music blaring in my ears, I

felt even lonelier. Would Kellum's "idea" change that?

I got out and wrapped my arms around myself to block the cold wind and hurried into the school.

Even though there were people in the hallway, no one greeted me. The dark gym had never looked so welcoming, and I slipped in, thankful for the low lighting. The sweetheart dance wasn't as special as homecoming or prom, but the freshman class had sprung for a DJ who'd brought a multi-colored light display and a smoke machine.

I made my way toward the opposite corner where I knew the food and drinks would be. I'd skipped dinner and hoped some food would settle my roiling stomach. My hands still shook from the run-in with my parents. The year and a half left until graduation might as well have been China for how impossibly far away it felt.

I poured a cup of punch and grabbed a chocolate chip cookie. While people danced to a fast song, I savored the sweet chips and the tangy coolness of punch on my tongue. I already felt better.

I scanned the room, looking for Kellum. He wasn't in one of the chairs lining the gym, so I looked toward the huddle of dancing bodies. Kellum danced with an enormous grin on his face, surrounded by a group of girls and guys. What could he possibly want with someone like me? Even hoping for a dance with him felt ridiculous when I had cookie crumbs and melted chocolate stuck to my fingers.

Three slow chords drifted over the speakers.

A slow song.

I saw Zack standing with his back to me, and he turned his head to either side, probably looking for someone to dance with. When saw me, he grinned a classic Zack smile, and then stuck out his hand.

I wiped my hands on a napkin and then placed on in his.

He led me to the middle of the gym and put his arms around my waist. As we spun in slow circles, Zack sang along to the song, out of key but totally happy. By the end of the first chorus, his glee had transferred to me like osmosis, and I wished I could keep it.

Through a giggle, I said, "I'm gonna miss you next year."

"I'll just be at Blackburn," he said.

"I guess an hour's not too far."

He dipped his head to the side. "Maybe you could come down and party with me sometime?"

"That would be awesome."

I only wished that would be a possibility—to go

out and have fun with friends, meet college boys, act like a happy teenager whose biggest worries were what to wear to school on Monday or passing a trig test.

"I'll make sure to text you," he said.

I nodded, pretending for the rest of the song a life like that could be my reality.

At the end of our dance, I walked to the edge of the floor and caught sight of one of the best-looking guys I'd ever seen. Rhett.

He stood behind Savannah with his arms around her waist, and Lorraine and Analeigh were next to them. That was what high school should be like. Good friends, a great guy, time to just be...yourself.

I gave them a small smile, and Analeigh waved me over. They complimented me on my shirt and the eye makeup I'd spend at least an hour working on. Then we danced. Rhett was a great dancer, and he practically had to drag Savannah out to the dance floor. She wasn't bad, but I could tell she was still nervous around him. Like she really liked him and didn't want to mess it up. I wouldn't have either.

After a few songs, I made a break for the punch table, and Cameron caught me en route.

"Do you want to dance?" he asked.

Saffron would not like that at all.

I looked around. "Where's your date?"

He grinned under his shaggy red hair and shrugged, brushing the ends with his shoulders. "Not here. Had to go to the bathroom."

I put my hand out for him to take, and he gripped it, turning and holding it over his shoulder on the way to dance.

As he pulled me to him, his cologne enveloped me like a cloud of pine needles and hay.

I waggled my eyebrows. "So that's who your poem was about?"

His cheeks flushed red under the strobe lights. "Maybe."

"I knew you wrote it!"

"Darn it!" He dropped his head back and let out an exasperated sigh. "You didn't know."

"I could tell."

He lifted his gaze so our eyes met, then he looked over his shoulder. "I still can't believe she agreed to come with me."

"I can."

A grateful smile touched his lips. "Thanks."

I nodded. "Any time."

I knew what that felt like—all the second-guessing, wondering if you were good enough. And Cameron shouldn't have to feel that way. We weren't close or anything, but he'd never been anything but nice to me.

After dancing with Cameron, I sat down in an open folding chair and watched couples spin around in varying degrees of intimacy. Savannah and Rhett looked so sweet together, swaying so close air couldn't exist between them.

Sheldon walked up to me and did a goofy spin move that somehow also incorporated a shoulder wave. I giggled, and he stuck out his hand for me to take. He waited while I put my cup down and stood up.

On the dance floor, he put his hands on my hips. "We haven't talked in forever."

I put my arms around his shoulders and agreed with him but didn't say more. We both knew the reason we hadn't talked.

He looked right at me, his blue eyes dancing right along with us. "It's been a rough year for our friend-ship, huh?"

If what we had could be referred to as a "friend-ship," then that was an understatement. He always found a way to be on the winning side of an argument, and it didn't matter whether it was my side or not. At least, it hadn't mattered when Shelby and Saffron were involved.

I stared down at the gym floor and the maroon line we swayed over. "I know you've been talking to Shelby about me. You've been listening to her talk crap about me, and you didn't even defend me. Or give me a chance to defend myself."

I immediately regretted confronting him about it. He was at least talking to me now. Even if I couldn't trust him, I needed a friend who lived in the same town as me. Any friend.

He nodded solemnly. "But just to let you know, nothing she said ever changed my opinion about you."

His story stunk just as badly as the Lanes' feed yard. I dropped my chin and raised my eyebrows.

"Really, Skye. It got to the point where I just didn't want to listen to her anymore. I was glad to help with her problems, but I feel bad that it hurt our friendship."

I looked away, blinking hard. "Like Shelby has any real problems. It's not like her friends ditched her, or she ruined her knee and any chance at college, or her parents set ridiculous curfews, or her sister doesn't talk to her anymore."

I sucked in a shaky breath because if I said another word I'd start bawling right there. My eyes stung, and my chest hurt more with each heartbeat.

Sheldon stopped dancing and dipped his knees, putting us almost at eye level. "I'm sorry things have been rough for you. If it makes you feel any better, Shelby's life isn't as perfect as she makes it out to be."

"It doesn't."

He pressed his lips together, and a line formed between his eyebrows. "It'll get better, Skye."

Empty promises.

The song lasted three times longer than I wanted it to. As I walked off of the dance floor, a stinging feeling lingered around my throat. Was Sheldon just being nice for the night, or did I actually have my friend back? And what were these "problems" Shelby had? Probably just some sob story to get him on her side.

Pathetic.

Another slow song came on. At first, I thought the DJ had played it by mistake, but he didn't change it.

I bumped into someone. "Oh, I'm sorry, I wasn't paying att—"

Kellum's dark eyes met mine, his lips almost in a smile. I wanted to run my fingers over them. To lift the corners. To let my heart slip out of my chest and land in his hands so someone other than me could take care of it.

"Wanna dance?" he asked.

Unable to find the right word, I nodded.

He walked to an empty spot, and I floated behind him like a balloon on a string, fighting to keep my face even, but I probably ended up somewhere between excited and terrified. Like the way someone looks in a skydiving photo.

Kellum turned and smiled at me like he didn't notice. He easily slipped his arms around my waist, linking his hands behind me. I did the same with my arms around his neck. I liked how he was taller, but not so tall I had to crane back to see him.

"How's it going?" he asked.

"Oh, pretty good." I aimed for casual, even though my stomach had missed the message and was doing the macarena. "You?"

He dipped his head side to side. "Not bad. Now."

I blushed and turned my head to the side so he wouldn't have a straight-on view of the grin splitting my face. How was I supposed to get through a whole dance with him looking at me like that? Through hooded eyes with a soft smile on his lips?

"So," I said.

"So." His smile sank through my eyes and landed on my heart, warming me from the inside out.

The lines to a T-Swift song played over the speakers, and I blushed at the reminder of how I'd embarrassed myself. At least she had words for every stage from I-think-he-might-like-me to this-son-of-a-you-know-what-is-going-to-die. Kellum and I were somewhere between.

I kept repeating Leslie's text in my mind. *Make him come to you.* Well, she hadn't told me what to do now that I had him here.

"So," he repeated. "About the note." He glanced at the small space between us.

"Yeah?"

"What do you think about doing something a little different?"

Saffron's voice sounded from behind me. "Looking good, Kell."

She and Cameron shuffled into view. I couldn't believe she was talking to Kellum while she was dancing with someone else. Especially since he hadn't asked her to Swirl. Poor Cameron.

The edges of Kellum's brown eyes tightened. "Thanks. You too."

Was it just me, or did his voice sound a little flat? Like he didn't really want to be talking to her?

"Back atcha, handsome," she said and literally winked.

I gave Cameron a pained look, but he didn't see it because he was staring at her. How could she do that to someone who so clearly adored her?

Kellum's shoulders lifted under my hands in a shrug.

Saffron flashed him a grin forged from the best dentistry her daddy could buy. "We better get back to dancing, huh?"

Kellum didn't respond, just turned back to face me.

In her final act of skullduggery, Saffron said, "You look really pretty, Skye."

I refused to return the compliment. It was clearly a lie anyway. My hair probably wasn't curled right, or my makeup wasn't heavy enough, or my thighs were too thick... A never-ending stream of my shortcomings flooded my mind while Kellum swayed across from me, probably eager for the song to fade out. No way would he want to carry out this "plan" when Saffron was so clearly into him.

I squinted at the clock on the wall, and a strobe light flashed over its face. 10:05. I'd need to leave after this dance anyway. I didn't need to make this night even worse by getting into a shouting match with my parents.

The final chords played, and I stepped away from Kellum. "Thanks."

Without waiting for his response, I walked to the edge of the gym, picked up my clutch bag and jacket, and headed into the hallway. I exited the school and stepped into the parking lot. The cool wind stung my exposed skin, and I shrugged on my jacket. My pickup probably wouldn't even be warm by the time I got home.

The school doors opened, but I kept my head down against the wind, in a march to the pickup.

"Skye. Wait up!"

Was that...

"Skye!"

Footsteps fell quickly until gravel crunched right behind me, and I turned to see Kellum standing an armlength away from me.

"Hey," he said, only slightly breathless.

A small laugh escaped my chest. "Hey?"

"Yeah. Hey." He took a step closer to me and put his hands on my shoulders. "I never got to ask you out."

"I...what?"

He bunched my curls in one hand, slowly pulled the ends of my hair from under my jacket, and smoothed it over my shoulder.

I shivered. Partly from the cold, mostly from his touch.

"Sign up for the ACT in Austin. They're having one at Upton. I'll take care of the rest."

He ran his hand from my shoulder down to my elbow and gave me a final lopsided smile. The kind that made me melt and freeze at the same time. And then he grinned. "I'm going to head inside. Want me to walk away slowly?"

Heat ran from my neck up my cheeks, and I covered my face. "Oh gosh."

I parted my fingers enough to see him grin.

"I wouldn't mind if you howled again," he said. "It was kinda cute."

Then he turned and jogged into the school. And I howled, like the idiot I was, because I'd do anything to have Kellum keep calling me cute.

I got into my pickup.

And we left to our lives that were different. But maybe, *maybe*, they were starting to come together. Just like I'd always wanted.

CHAPTER TWELVE

I MADE it home a few minutes before curfew.

Mom stood by the microwave, a bag of popcorn popping loudly. Dad's snores sounded from the couch, first soft then loud, loud, louder.

"Cutting it close," she said.

I seriously didn't have it in me to fight. I was so happy right now. I shrugged. "Inch is as good as a mile."

She folded her arms over her chest. "How was the dance?"

"It was great. Thanks for letting me go."

Her features softened in surprise. "Well...you're welcome. Want some popcorn?"

Its buttery scent filled my nostrils, but I shook my head. I had a few unopened texts from Andrew, and I still had a lot of fantasizing to do about Kellum and our wedding day and how I'd tell our future 2.8 children the way he asked me on our first date.

I wasn't crazy or anything.

"Goodnight," she said.

I gave her a side hug. "Night."

In my room, I took off my brace and stretched out my leg. Now, without the distraction of Kellum or pounding music, I could feel how tired and achy my knee was. Standing and dancing had taken its toll.

I shimmied out of my dance clothes—apparently, they'd done the trick—and slipped on some shorts and a t-shirt for the night. I still felt like dancing, but not the awkward there-are-other-people-around kind. The I'm-so-freaking-happy-and-just-need-to-get-it-out variety.

I did a spin and landed on my back on my bed, bringing my phone with me. Time to check my messages.

Andrew: Hey.

Andrew: Missed texting you tonight.

Andrew: How was the dance?

My heart fell for reasons I didn't understand. Shouldn't I have been floating on a cloud?

Me: I missed talking to you too.

Me: The dance was great. Made it home two minutes before curfew, so I count that as a win.

Andrew: It's not even 11... When was your curfew?

Me: :(

Me: 10:30.

Andrew: Are you serious?

Me: YUP. Wish I wasn't.

Andrew: You're a junior, right? I haven't had a 10:30 curfew since... Maybe like 8th grade when my parents had to pick me up.

I rolled over on my stomach and glared at my phone.

Me: Rub it in why don't you?

But that seemed a little harsh, so I sent him an LOL too.

Andrew: That just seems crazy to me. Like...do your parents let you date or anything?

Define "anything."

Me: Depends on the day.

Andrew: What about today? ;)

I sat straight up in my bed and stared at the screen.

What. Did. That. Mean?

And how on earth did I respond to that?

Me: Depends on who's asking. :)

Andrew: I'll keep that in mind. ;)

What was with all these winky faces? I had a hard enough time deciphering his words, much less the cryptic yellow emojis.

Andrew: So, do you like slow dancing or fast dancing better?

Me: Slow. Definitely.

Andrew: Why?

Me: I have two left feet. Unless I'm getting the directions, I'm kind of hopeless haha

Andrew: That's cute.

Me: :)

Me: What's your favorite?

Andrew: Depends on the day. ;)

Me: Ha. Ha. Ha.

Me: Really.

Andrew: Depends on who I'm dancing with.

Andrew: Really.

Me: Yeah?

Andrew: Yeah, like, I'm not going to slow dance with Roberto. That would just be weird.

Me: And here I thought you were going to say something sweet. :P

Andrew: I wasn't finished.

My heart stopped, waiting for his next text.

Andrew: The best kind of relationship is where

you can do both. Have fun fast dancing, making goofy faces, then stop and just...be. Like, it doesn't matter what music's playing or who's there or if you're at a dance or in the living room. It just matters who you're dancing with.

My fingers hovered over the screen. I didn't know what to say or how to take it or if he was thinking about dancing with me like I was thinking about dancing with him. And I shouldn't have been. Hadn't Kellum—AKA dream guy I'd been drooling over for the last year—just asked me out? And if my dreams were coming true, why did I feel so conflicted?

Andrew: I better get to bed. Church and then homework tomorrow.

Andrew: Goodnight, beautiful. Sweet dreams.

My hand covered my mouth. Because I'd gotten a goodnight text like that, and I hadn't even tried. Hadn't been anything other than myself.

CHAPTER THIRTEEN

THE LIGHT in my room flicked on, and I threw my forearm over my eyes. They felt crusty and hot since I'd been up so late the night before, tossing and turning and fretting about cute guys and perfect texts.

"Up and at 'em," Dad said.

"Why?" I croaked.

"More work out at the Lanes'. Branch said Howard thought they might have something for you to work on."

I pulled my arm back and sat up. "Dad, Dr. Pike said I need to be really careful with my knee."

"Branch was out working three days after his surgery. You've been laying around long enough. You're getting lazy."

Anger flared up in my chest. Lazy? Had he seen me up every morning doing my exercises? Watched me spend my entire weights class biking? "What do they even want me to do?"

His lip twitched into a sneer. "We'll find you something."

That meant I'd be standing around for hours on end handing him tools and gritting my teeth against stupid things Branch said about women who definitely were not his wife. But I knew better than to argue with Dad when he wanted me to work with him. And at least Rhett would be there.

"Fine," I snapped. "I'm getting up."

"I'll be in the pickup," he said and slammed the door behind him.

Great. Perfect way to start out my one day off—way too early and still late.

I threw on some work jeans, my brace, a sweater, and boots, then worked my hair into a (really) messy bun held back by a thick headband. I didn't have time for makeup, so I splashed water on my face and hoped Rhett wouldn't get close enough to see the dark circles below my eyes.

I went into the kitchen, grabbed a travel mug, and stopped by the coffee pot. Empty.

Great. The least he could have done was save a little bit for me.

Like promised, Dad was waiting in the pickup. I opened the door to my side, shoved the old magazines and other junk over, and sat down.

Dad took a deep drink from his mug, then set it down and backed out of the drive. I stared out the window. No wonder Liz left this place and never came back, never called. That was what I'd be doing the second I graduated high school.

We rode in silence, listening to classic rock punctuated by ads for grain and cell phone service on the radio. Eventually, we drove under that metal sign and up to the shop building. It looked completely finished from the outside, but I knew looks could be deceiving.

Branch's pickup sat in the drive, and a few guys stood around the pickup. I recognized Rhett's broad shoulders, Branch's spindly frame. Howard had to be the other one.

Dad parked next to Branch's pickup, and I got out, ready to be away from him.

Rhett smiled at me under his ball cap and nodded. "Hey, stranger. Haven't seen you in a while."

My cheeks heated under the looks Branch and

Howard gave me. Why did it feel so weird to see guys my age when adults were around?

I gave him a little laugh. "What's it been? Eight hours?"

"Give or take."

Howard nodded at me. "Morning, Skye."

I smiled at him. "Good morning."

Branch greeted Dad. "Finally got her out of bed, huh?"

Dad mumbled something into his mustache then said, "So, we ready to get to work?"

Howard hooked his thumbs in his pockets. "We need to insulate the shed and get the electrical done. Branch told me you were certified, Bill?"

Dad nodded. "Sure am."

Howard nodded too. "Well, we can start with that."

"You said you might have something for Skye?" Dad asked.

"Yeah, we need to get some temporary fence up. I thought Skye could ride along with Rhett and help him out."

Oh my gosh, please. That would be a million times better than hanging around Dad and Branch a second longer.

Dad shrugged. "Sure."

Rhett jerked his thumb over his shoulder. "Okay, let's head out."

Without saying goodbye to Dad, I followed Rhett to a rusty pickup with a giant roll of smooth wire on the back. They meant business.

Rhett stopped at a cooler on the back. "Want some water? Gatorade?"

"Gatorade," I said.

He tossed me a red bottle over the bed.

"Thank you so much," I said.

He gave me a crooked grin and got in, and I did too.

"Seriously," I said. "Dad didn't leave any coffee for me this morning, and I'm dying."

He laughed. "I've got you covered." He handed me a thermos, then flipped open a lunch box sitting between us full of sandwiches, chips, and what looked like brownies. "Mom stocked this up for us."

"Rhett... I think I might be in love with your mom."

He laughed and hit the lid shut. "Awkward."

I shifted in my seat and opened the thermos. As he pulled out, I carefully poured myself a cup and took a sip. The hot liquid glided down my throat, and its rich smell hit my nose. I already felt better.

"Seriously."

He laughed again.

"So what are we doing?" I asked.

He drove with one hand on the steering wheel and put the other across the seat behind me. "We put up temp—temporary—fence to let the cattle graze on a pasture for a short while. Usually on a wheat field or corn stalks or something like that. Since the cows are calving—having their babies—they're already set. This'll be for the steers we're trying to fatten up."

I nodded, loving the way Rhett talked about the ranch. Sure and confident and...passionate. Like he loved working there.

"Har and Mom are out tagging calves now, actually. We might see them on the way to the field."

I drained the rest of my cup and twisted the lid back on. "Sounds good. Um. Rhett?"

He glanced at me. "Yeah?"

"My knee... It's not really 100 percent yet. This isn't going to be hard on it, will it?"

His hazel eyes softened even more in the golden morning light. "Nah, I'll have you drive while I put the posts in. No worries."

Relieved, I smiled. "Thanks."

"Hey," he said and pointed out the windshield. "There they are."

Near a fence, Harleigh and her mom knelt over a small black shape.

Rhett slowed and drove closer to them. When he got a few feet away from the fence, he put the pickup in park. "Come on."

He got out, and I followed him to the barbed-wire fence. Now that we were closer, I could see the small calf on the ground. Harleigh held it down, and Rhett's mom snapped a tag in its ear.

The calf bellered, and a nearby cow stomped at the ground.

"It's okay, mama," Harleigh said in a low voice.

She got off the calf, and it walked all bandy-legged back to its mom. It's silky black hair shined.

"Hey," Rhett said. "Wanted to show Skye the calves."

Deena smiled at me. "Hey, there."

Harleigh wiped her hands on her pants. "What do you think?"

I grinned, my eyes still on the calf, now nursing. "So cool."

Harleigh grinned, too, following my eyes. I'd never seen her light up like that. "Calving season's the best time of the year."

Deena scoffed. "Sure, if you like working eighty hours a week."

Harleigh shrugged. "I don't mind."

I stepped a little closer to the fence and gripped the smooth place between the rusty barbs. "How many calves will you have?"

"About three-fifty," Rhett said.

I gazed over the pasture, not believing each of the little black dots in the distance could be a cow ready to have her own calf. In the hazy morning light, it looked like something out of a magazine. "Wow."

Deena wiped at her forehead. "Yep. Lots of work to do. At least ten dropped calves last night." She pointed at the one nursing behind her. "That was number two."

Rhett nodded. "Well, we'll let you guys get to it."

We walked back to the pickup and got in. On our way to the field, I stared out the window, trying to catch glimpses of the calves and their moms, loving the way they bandied around and how the cows kept close to their babies. Beautiful.

The vehicle slowed, and Rhett steered us off the road into a pasture.

I stared at the green expanse. "Is this it?"

Rhett nodded then came to a stop and put the pickup in park. "Okay, so here's the deal. I'll put those posts back there"—he jerked his thumb toward the pickup bed where hundreds of metal rods lay

—"in the ground every fifteen feet or so. I'll drive one in, hop in, and tell you when to stop. Sound good?"

I nodded. "Easy peasy, right?"

A smile cracked his face. "Right."

For the next couple hours, we drove along the pasture boundary, Rhett driving posts into the ground. Since he was constantly in and out, I kept the heater cranked against the February chill. But even for how cold it was outside, Rhett had sweat dripping down his face when we finished.

After the last post was in the ground, Rhett extended his hand across the cab. I high-fived him.

"That was the easy part," he said.

I stared at him, his sweating face. "Seriously?"

He laughed. "Nah. We just have to string the wire now."

More driving. More instructions from Rhett. And, finally, a fence with smooth, electric wire.

"Phew," Rhett said, settling into the passenger side.

"Wanna trade spots so we can go back?"

He leaned his head back and looked over at me. "Not really."

I gave him a confused smile. "Yeah?"

"Let's just..." He looked around the cab, and his eyes landed on the lunchbox. He picked it up. "Have lunch? Hang out? I mean, it has to be better than hanging around that dipshit."

My mouth fell open, and a half laugh, half gasp, half snort came out.

Rhett cracked up. "What was that?"

My cheeks flamed, and I covered my mouth. "I wasn't expecting that!"

He laughed. "Me neither."

I hit his shoulder. "Come on."

He pressed his lips together, his shoulders shaking, and I hit him again.

He laughed out loud again, but finally quieted, his cheeks still red. "Seriously, though. I know Branch drives you crazy."

"He's not the only one."

Rhett playfully narrowed his eyes. "Hey, now."

I shrugged then laughed. "Just kidding."

"Uh huh." He tilted his head toward me. "But seriously."

"I know. And of course he's Dad's best friend."

Rhett trained his eyes on the lunchbox and opened it. "Yeah. So, turkey or ham?"

"Turkey."

He handed me a sandwich, and I peeled back the foil. Usually I felt awkward eating in front of guys—especially cute ones—but knowing Rhett was dating

Savannah made it easier. I sank my teeth into the sandwich and chewed slowly, enjoying the country song playing through the radio and the sound of wind against the cab.

"So," Rhett said, "What's new in the life of Skye?"

I looked down at my knee, thinking about all that had changed in the last month. "I mean, this brace is pretty new."

He reached out and touched the smooth metal. "How's recovery going?"

Even though he wasn't touching me, I still wanted to shiver. "Slowly."

He nodded. "Takes time."

"Too much time."

He lifted one corner of his mouth. "Any developments in the dating department? You and Kellum looked pretty cozy at the dance last night. I saw him follow you out." He made some kissing sounds.

My cheeks heated, and my stomach twisted at the thought of how Kellum had played with my hair in the parking lot. "He asked me out."

"Killer." Rhett's lips lifted into a full-fledged grin, and for the first time, he felt more like a friend than an insanely handsome movie star I somehow got to work with. Still, were we seriously talking about guys?

I laughed. "Hardly. I don't even know what we're doing."

His brows furrowed. "What do you mean? When are y'all going out?"

I shrugged. "Monday. He said to sign up for the ACT in Austin."

"And your parents are okay with that?"

I tugged my lips into a frown. "If by 'okay' you mean they have no idea about it and I'm not planning on telling them, then..."

A mischievous grin this time. "Nice."

"I mean, I'd rather be able to tell them, but after what happened with James..."

Part of me was scared to bring it up, scared to see how many people James had told about my dad basically cussing him out and threatening to beat the crap out of him, if not worse.

Rhett waved his hand dismissively. "James is a chickenshit anyway."

My chest lightened. "What's with you and all the 'shits' today?"

He laughed. "I don't know. You're the one bringing 'em all up!"

"Sure."

Rhett crumpled up his foil and dropped it in the lunchbox. "Any other prospects?"

"Usually, no, but in this bizarre twist of fate..." I sighed, thinking of Andrew. "Kind of."

"'Kind of'?"

I picked at the Velcro on my brace. "There's this guy... From Woodman."

"What's his name? I might know him."

"Andrew?"

Rhett stared across the field. "Hmm." He shook his head. "What's he like?"

My lips lifted. "You really want to hear about how cute he is?"

He shrugged. "Eh, why not?"

I stared out the windshield, too shy to look at him. "Um. He's nice. Really nice. And smart—like all of his texts are spelled out and use proper grammar and all that stuff. He's funny, but not in an obvious kind of way, like he reads the situation and knows how to make people smile." Knows how to make me smile. "And. Well. He's not like Kellum-level hot, but he's not bad to look at either." I looked over at Rhett. "Sorry, is that weird?"

Rhett shook his head. "I mean, kind of, but it's cool." He laughed. "So you like both of them."

I nodded. "I think the real problem is that they both might like me."

I'd expected Rhett to laugh, but he just nodded. "So you might have to make a choice. What's your gut telling you?"

I groaned. "That I'll probably screw something up before I ever even get close to choosing."

"Hey," he said, his voice hard. "Don't you ever discount yourself. These guys have every reason to like you, but if you're constantly questioning yourself, they will too."

I looked down at my brace. What he was saying made sense, but... "Every reason to like me?"

Rhett grinned and rolled his head back. "Come on, Skye."

"What?" I lifted my hands. "It's not like guys have been lining up to get themselves a piece of this."

He laughed. "A piece of this Skye?"

I rolled my eyes. "Something like that."

"You're beautiful, Skye, and not in the cute, little girl kind of way. And you're funny—easy to talk to. Any time I'm around you, I have this feeling like..." he reached out and put a rough hand on the back of my neck, running his thumb across the hair over my temple. "Like you have a million thoughts going through your mind, and it's impossible not to wonder what they are."

My breath caught in my throat, and tears prickled my eyes. "Really?"

He gave me a friendly smile and nodded. "Look, here's how you tell. The person you should choose—if it's one of these guys—he'll be the person who makes you feel like you can be the best version of yourself. When you're with that person, something will just...click, and it'll be like you can see the future and it's you and that person, but the you you want to be, not the you you are now. And he won't make you wonder if you're good enough or if he likes you. It will be there, plain as day. No games, no doubts, just you and him."

I swallowed back a lump in my throat. Had I ever even felt like that? "Have you felt like that? With Savannah?"

Keeping his eyes on mine, he nodded. "The second I met her."

"Wow," I breathed.

"Can I tell you something?"

This time, I nodded.

"I think I'm going to marry her someday, and that scares the hell outta me."

I couldn't fathom feeling that way about

someone and having them return the feeling. Sure, I wanted to have someone who would be there for me —with me—through everything. Someone who I could just *be* with, like Andrew said the night before. More than anything.

But getting there? That was the trouble.

CHAPTER FOURTEEN

I WENT to school early Monday morning to use a computer in the library. Usually I only did that if I had homework that needed faster Internet than we had at home, but today I had to sign up for the ACT.

I filled out my information, answered all the career aptitude questions, and when it came time to select a location... I froze. I couldn't ask my parents for permission, but I couldn't not go. I had to go.

Taking in a deep breath, I selected Upton University as the location and triple-clicked "submit" before I could talk myself out of it. Chances to date your dream guy didn't come up every day, let alone every lifetime, and I wasn't going to miss mine.

Still, acid nerves ate at my stomach the entire morning. Mrs. Valor lectured all through A&P, and

Kellum and I sat in our usual spots, not beside each other. Other than a few stolen smiles, Kellum didn't treat me any differently. Weights would be the real test where I would learn if I'd really just been dreaming.

I approached the locker room and heard Rachel and Shelby's voices up the stairs. They sounded hushed, which only made me want to listen in more.

"I got an offer at A&M," Rachel said. "Partial scholarship. They'll probably redshirt me the first year." She sighed.

"Are you going to sign with them?" Shelby asked.

Everyone had been guessing where Rachel would go to college next year, but my bet was she'd go to a community college nearby. She loved her family way too much to move away so quickly.

"I don't know, I mean, do I really want to dedicate my life to practice and sit on the bench for five years?"

"Yeah," Shelby said. "I don't know. I haven't heard back from the coach at Upton yet. Hopefully any day now."

"You think they'll give you an offer?" Rachel asked.

"I don't know." Her voice hardened. "I sent him

some film, and the coach asked me if our libero was a senior."

Rachel sucked in a breath. "Yikes."

A smile found my lips. A division one coach was asking about me?

Then I looked down at the white brace on my knee, and my heart fell. Even if I did get released in time to play, how much ground would I have to make up?

I took advantage of the quiet moment and stepped into the locker room, acting like I hadn't heard a word. "Hey."

Rachel smiled at me. "Hey, Skye."

Shelby turned away and shut her locker.

"Hey Shelby," I said. I didn't know why. We'd settled comfortably into a routine of not talking to each other.

She glared at me then walked out.

I couldn't feel sorry for her. Not even a little. Maybe if she'd spent more time building herself up instead of tearing me down, she wouldn't be waiting on an offer that might not come.

Rachel grimaced at me, and I shrugged. Whatever. I had bigger things to worry about, like the fact that Kellum was probably in the gym already, wearing a cut-off shirt that showed off every muscle between his ribs.

At the memory of him touching my hair and running his hand down my arm, my skin tingled.

"See you up there?" Rachel asked.

"Sure."

She left, and I changed in silence. I stopped by the mirror and checked my makeup. Usually, I didn't wear this much, but I needed to make sure Kellum didn't change his mind about taking me out. A little of my mascara had flecked off and landed underneath my eyes. I brushed it off and practiced my smile in the mirror.

Eh. Good enough.

I walked up the stairs, took a deep breath, and stepped into the gym. The distance across the court to the small group of students felt like an eternity, and all of a sudden, I felt self-conscious about the way I walked. Was it too fast? Too slow? Stiff?

Finally, finally, I made it across. Kellum and Zack were joking about something, as usual, and Coach Rokey led us to the weight room.

"Before everyone gets started, I want to talk to you about something," Rokey said.

Our group gathered around him, a few people standing, a few sitting on the benches. Across our loose circle, Kellum's eyes caught mine. He lifted a corner of his mouth, and I smiled back before looking to the ground. I'd have to get over this blushing, jittery thing by next Saturday.

"As you know, the state weightlifting competition is coming up, and I want to start making decisions about who we'll bring. I want everyone to come weigh in, and we'll talk about it from there."

I froze in place, feeling instantly sick to my stomach. Nothing made a Monday better than getting weighed in front of your crush.

Rokey clapped his hands. "Okay, line up."

He picked up a clipboard from his desk and walked over to the scale. The guys queued up first, and then us girls. I stood only a few people behind Kellum, ahead of Shelby and Rachel.

Rokey weighed each of the guys, saying their weight out loud and then writing it down.

The closer I got to the scale, the tauter my nerves grew. Would Kellum still want to date me after he heard my weight? Saffron had to weigh 110, 120 maybe. I had at least forty-five pounds on her. Maybe more.

"Skye," Rokey said, and I stepped on the scale.

He tapped the top slider over, all the way to the edge, but it still didn't level out.

I let out a quiet sigh and closed my eyes for a second.

He moved the bigger slider over then nudged the top across.

"175," he announced.

My stomach turned, and my cheeks flamed. He'd said that so loudly.

"Rachel," he said.

I didn't hear her weight, didn't hear anything other than my heart pounding in my ears. I was up twenty pounds. Out of my weight class. I weighed only two pounds less than Kellum, and I stood at least five inches shorter than him.

I sat down on a bench and rubbed my temples. How had I let this happen?

Someone sat next to me, and I glanced over at them. Kellum.

He rested his elbows on his knees and twisted his head toward mine. "Hey."

My stomach bounced, and despite the turmoil in my mind, I found myself smiling. "Hey."

He faced forward, and I gave myself a quarter of a second to take in his profile. Long lashes, dark eyes, sharp jaw, curved lips.

"Okay," Rokey began. He read down the list and said which weight class everyone was in, whether he thought they would be competitive at state, and whether they should try to gain or lose.

"Skye," he said. "You're in the power class now."

I cringed. Those were the girls who dedicated their lives to weights. They were heavy, strong, and way out of my league.

"You'd only be able to compete in bench press, and unless you can get down about...twenty pounds, I don't think it would be worth your time to go."

Tears stung my eyes, and I nodded, blinking them back.

While Rokey talked to Rachel and Shelby, Kellum bumped my shoulder. "You okay?"

I tried to smile, but my lips faltered, and I took a deep breath. "I don't know."

He rubbed my back, but it only made the tears swell. I hated how someone being nice to me, comforting me, had that effect.

"It'll be okay," he whispered.

I looked at him, a small line of tears along my lashes. "Will it?"

"If you have anything to do with it."

Rokey had the class start lifting, and I went to the corner of the room to work through my rehab exercises. They hurt. I was weak. I couldn't wait for this day to be over.

Finally, Rokey said we could go.

After changing, we all went to the lunch room and sat down together. Kellum sat to my right, Rachel on my left, and Zack and Shelby sat across from us. We'd sat together before, but today felt different. Like maybe we were on the edge of something I'd been dreaming of for a long, long time.

The conversation turned to state weight lifting. Good feelings gone.

Rachel asked Shelby if she was going to go.

"I might. At least I wouldn't have to lose weight or anything." Shelby's lip curled. "What did Coach say you had to lose to compete, Skye? Like thirty-five pounds?"

I gaped at her. Seriously?

She smiled at me, all sweet, like she genuinely cared.

I glanced at the food on my tray. Yet another reason Kellum could choose someone better.

"Twenty, right?" Shelby pressed. "Looks like you're not going to try and lose it then? I mean, look at all those carbs. You're having *two* rolls?"

I gave her a warning glance.

She lifted her fork and waved it around as she talked. "I totally admire how you're fine just letting yourself go. I wish I could just eat whatever I wanted without worrying about how much weight I'd gained."

I opened my mouth, still not sure what I would say, but knowing I needed to say something to put this smug piece of crap in her place.

Kellum lifted his milk. "I like a girl who eats."

Zack tapped his carton to Kellum's. "Here, here." He winked. "Gotta have something to hold onto."

Rachel laughed. "Please."

Kellum kept his carton up. He was waiting for me.

With a grateful smile, I tapped my carton to his. "Cheers."

He held my eyes. "Cheers."

CHAPTER FIFTEEN

FOR THE REST of the week, Kellum and I continued our dance of more-than-friends-but-not-quite-lovers during the day, and Andrew and I texted for hours after school. Every time I talked to them, Rhett's words hung in the back of my mind. If it ever came down to choosing, how would I decide?

Saturday didn't leave me time to consider it too much, because Mr. Yen added another event to my schedule—policy debate—and the meet lasted most of the day. At home, I fell into bed and slept until ten the next morning.

I got up and went to the kitchen to grab something for breakfast. Mom sat in front of the fridge, the door open and its entire contents on the ground around her. She dipped a sponge into a bucket of soapy water.

Mom didn't clean often, but sometimes she got into one of these moods. Which meant I'd be her personal helper for hours on end.

I turned and stepped as softly as I could toward my room. I could go without food for a few hours.

"Skye!" Mom called.

I cringed but wiped it from my face before I turned around. "Morning, Mom."

"Cleaning day," she said like I couldn't tell from all the crap laying around her. "This house is a pigsty."

I couldn't argue. She always left her clothes on the bathroom floor, Dad never put his dishes in the sink when he was done with them, and dust somehow worked its way to cover every surface. Of course, that didn't matter much from the comfort of my room.

"I was just gonna grab some breakfast," I said.

"Ah." She lifted a nearly empty carton of milk. "The date on this says yesterday, but it's still good. I smelled it. Can you finish it off?"

My stomach soured, but I couldn't argue. When Mom got into one of these moods, anything could set her off.

I took the milk and poured myself a bowl of off-brand cereal. Something coated in sugar that tasted like crunched up corn straight from the field.

I took it to the table and ate while Mom aggressively scrubbed at the fridge. It probably hadn't been given a good cleaning in a couple months.

As soon as Mom heard my spoon scraping the bottom of the bowl, she was on me to start cleaning. First order of business? Sweeping and then hand-scrubbing the floors because "a mop just doesn't do as good as elbow grease."

For hours, we deep cleaned the house. From rearranging every can in the pantry to wiping down baseboards and cleaning the oven, we did it all. Of course, Dad was nowhere to be found and would come home to a clean house without even having to lift a finger.

Finally, Mom ran out of things for us to clean.

I dropped onto the couch in the living room, exhausted.

She took her keys off the hook. "I'm going grocery shopping."

"'Kay," I said.

She left, and the heater kicked on. The warm air on my face felt nice. My eyelids grew heavy, so heavy

I couldn't lift them, and I slipped into a dreamless nap.

A slamming door woke me up.

I sat up, rubbing my eyes. What was going on?

Mom dropped two bags full of groceries on the floor and stood with her hands on her hips. "Why are you always laying around the house?" she asked, her voice hard.

When my mind connected the pieces, I stared at her, shocked. "What are you talking about?"

"I've been gone for four hours, and you're laying in exactly the same place you were when I left."

"I took a nap."

She rolled her eyes and nodded slowly. "You don't say?" She pointed at the corner of her chin. "You've got some drool there."

I pressed my lips together and swiped at my face.

"You're always here," she accused.

"What?" Where was all of this coming from?

"It's like I can't ever get away from you."

She acted like it was my choice to be stuck in the house all the time. Like I didn't live here. "Maybe I don't go out because every time I ask, you and Dad say I can't go or give me a ridiculous curfew. Like 10:30 for a dance that ends at midnight."

"I'm tired of you being around! All you do is lay around and eat."

"I'm injured!"

"Oh please," she said. "It's just an excuse to be lazy and get fat."

"Did you just call me fat?"

"If the shoe fits."

I gaped at her, unable to even put into words how awful I felt, how her words hit me like a right hook to the gut. I'd expected it from Shelby, but from my own mother?

"Just get out," she said.

"Fine, I'll leave."

By the time I got to my pickup in the driveway I was crying. My gas tank was empty, and Mom and Dad hated paying for gas, and I had no idea what I was supposed to do or who I was supposed to do it with.

I thought about texting Anika, but something stopped me. I called Andrew instead and started driving to the gas station. I needed his sunshine smile.

He answered, his happiness to hear from me clear in the way he said hello.

"Hey, do you want to meet in Roderdale and

hang out?" I asked. "Just as friends?" I added because I didn't want to sound too needy.

I didn't think asking him to come would be a big deal since we had been talking so much, but it would be about half an hour for him to drive, and I hoped his parents would let him see me.

"Let me go ask my mom real quick," he said.

"Sure."

I heard static on the phone as he set it down.

Then silence for a few minutes.

"Hey, uh, Skye? Still there?"

"Yeah, what'd she say?"

"She said I could come." I could hear the smile in his voice again, and I couldn't wait to see it in person.

"Awesome! Are you leaving soon?"

"Yeah, I'll see you soon."

I used the credit card we had for gas to fill up the tank and drove to Roderdale, listening to music the whole way, imagining what Andrew and I could do in a town small enough to miss if you sneezed on your way through.

I stopped in the park and waited. Instead of getting out, I pulled a notebook out of my purse and started writing about a girl with a bionic knee who used it to defeat an evil slug with acid slime trailing behind it.

Andrew showed up right before the girl poured an Empire State Building-sized bucket of salt on the villain.

He got out of his car, and I did the same. As I walked toward him, I took him in, admired the dark blue sweater that made his eyes look as fluid as a melting cerulean crayon.

Apparently, jeans and blue tops were the trend.

I gripped the ends of my sleeves from inside my sweater. "We match."

He looked down like he was confused, and then let out the happiest laugh I'd ever heard in my life. "Great minds think alike," he said and gave me a side-arm hug.

I melted into his warmth, and when he let me go, it immediately felt like something was missing.

"It's freezing out here." He rubbed his hands together against the cold.

I nodded. "So, where to?"

"You hungry?"

My stomach practically jumped at the words. All I'd had was cereal and expired milk.

We decided to pick something up at the gas station and come back to the park. Andrew paid the bill.

Back in his car, I said, "You didn't have to do that. It's not like we're on a date or anything."

He handed me a box of Milk Duds. "No, but we could make it one."

Butterflies that usually only took flight when Kellum was around swooped through my insides.

I popped a Milk Dud in my mouth and let the sticky caramel lock my mouth shut. I didn't need to say anything dumb and mess this up. Whatever it was that I was messing up.

He parked next to my pickup and let his car idle.

I broke my jaw apart and swallowed. "So, what do you want to do?"

He took a sip from his slushy. "Wanna play firsts?"

"Firsts?"

"Yeah, it's like twenty questions, but instead you ask about all your firsts."

I thought it over. "I'm game."

He grinned. "Okay, I'll go. First broken bone?"

I groaned. "I tripped over something when I was helping Dad at a worksite and fractured my wrist."

He raised his eyebrows. "Beauty and poise? I like that."

I laughed and hit his arm. "First time you lied

about being sick so you wouldn't have to go to school."

"Never." He shook his head. "I always liked going to school."

I leaned my head back and rolled my eyes. "You're kidding me."

"Nope."

"Then there's still time to corrupt you."

"I think I'm up for that." He laughed. "First time you drank."

"Oh, Dad's friend gave me a beer to try when I was like twelve. It was awful."

"No, like, first time you drank with friends."

I shook my head. "Nope. First time you...had food poisoning."

"Wait, wait, wait." He held up his hands. "You mean you've never been drunk, right, not that you've never drank?"

I shook my head. "My parents don't really let me out often, and I'm not totally crazy about what drinking does to people."

"I get that. Okay, first time I had food poisoning. I was outside, and we had a pet rabbit—Einstein— that ate grass, and I thought it would be cool to be a bunny, so I ate grass too. I was so sick. Like for days."

I laughed. "Nice one, Einstein."

He wiggled his nose at me like a rabbit, and I laughed harder. Talking to him came so easily.

"First time you realized what you looked like."

I took a drink from my slushy and thought back to that moment. "I have an older sister. She's a few years older than me, and she was getting ready to go to a pool party with her friends, and the only swimsuit my parents had for her was too big, so they had to use a bread twist to tie it back and keep it secure. She cried so hard she made herself sick, and Mom and Dad got mad, so she didn't go. I think she was in fourth grade, and I was in first. And I hadn't ever really thought about what I wore or anything before that, but after..." I sighed. I hadn't stopped thinking about it since.

Wind buffeted around his car. The sky was dark blue, but inky black tree branches swayed across it.

"Hey, Andrew?"

He leaned back against his door. "Hey, Skye?"

I smiled, but paused, wondering if I really wanted to ask the question that had been burning on my mind. About what he meant by saying we could make this a date. I'd had my share of heartbreak, and I knew the higher you got your hopes, the harder you fell. Sure, soaring was nice, but rooting yourself in reality was the only way to keep from falling.

But I wasn't ready to stop flying now.

I took a breath. "First kiss you had in this car?"

A smile lingered on his sweet lips. The kind that promised good things were coming.

He shook his head slowly one way, then the other. "First time you thought about kissing me."

He moved closer, leaning across the console, and paused inches from me. The street lamps cast a shine in his eyes, almost all pupil and thin blue iris.

My breath caught, but I couldn't answer. Couldn't tell him I'd been thinking about his kiss since the first time I'd seen him smile.

I closed the gap, and my lips landed on his—curious, soft, tentative. They felt just like I'd expected, but totally different at the same time.

His fingers wound through the hair at the back of my neck, and he held me close, as close as two people could be with two jumbo drinks and a center console between them.

We broke apart, but he stayed close, his soft breath landing in puffs along my wet lips. His eyes slid to my mouth, and he came back for more, deepening our kiss until I didn't know where my lips ended and his began.

I stopped counting time by seconds or minutes and started counting by the soft stroke of his fingers in my hair and the glance of his lips against mine. He smiled against my mouth, and I smiled against his, and we were smiling and kissing, and it was beautiful and fun and awkward, and everything a first kiss should be but somehow more.

I drove the entire way home with a smile plastered on my face. The last time I'd been this happy I was picking up my white libero jersey. I just hoped this didn't end as badly.

When I pulled up to the house at 10:30, all the lights were still on, and Dad's truck was finally back in the driveway. No one had called me since I'd been out, but that didn't really mean much.

As I got closer to the house, I started hearing shouting. Indistinguishable at first, but then louder, louder, until I could hear their yelling match just as clearly outside the door as if I was standing in the room with them.

"You think you can just stay out all weekend with your friends? We have a daughter!"

A glass shattered, and I cringed.

Dad roared, "Don't act like you even care! You ran our last one off, and Skye's going to do exactly the same thing. Just you wait." His words slurred, even with the force used to say them.

"Only because she's sick of dealing with a scumbag like you!" Mom yelled back.

My heart fell from the silver-lined cloud it had been resting on and landed somewhere around the earth's core. They could argue like this for hours.

"You think it's me they're running away from? Where's Skye? Huh? Where was I this weekend? Trying to get away from you!"

I pressed my fingers into my temples and rubbed.

Mom let a string of profanities fly his direction, and Dad slung them right back.

She changed tactics again. "Were you out with Jana?"

"Are you shitting me?" Dad yelled. "Why would I run off looking for another woman? I can't even stand one!"

"It was Riley, then. Don't even lie to me!"

Metal clanging sounded. Pots and pans being thrown and landing on the floor, bouncing once or twice. "STOP! STOP STOP STOP!"

"OOOH!" Mom screamed. "YOU PIECE OF—"

More pans being thrown.

"GET OUT!" She yelled.

Dad's voice grew so quiet I barely heard him say, "Thought you'd never ask."

His heavy footsteps sounded, and I hurried off the porch. I ran around the side of the house so he wouldn't see me on his way to the pickup. Dad wasn't above taking his anger out on Liz when she was here, and now I was the only one left.

Dad stumbled down the sidewalk, got into his pickup, fired up the engine, peeled out, and drove down the road.

I shook my head, wishing he'd never come back. But I knew he would in a few days. And all would be forgotten, but never forgiven.

CHAPTER SIXTEEN

ANDREW: Good morning, beautiful. How did you sleep?

I blinked my dry lids at the message. My heart had taken up new residence in the pit of my stomach, and I'd only been able to sleep maybe a few hours after I heard my mom cry herself to sleep. Maybe.

But I didn't want that to be my reality. I wanted to be like a normal teen, going on dates, stealing kisses, and waking up in a home that didn't have pots and pans we'd worked so hard to clean and organize scattered around the floor.

Me: Amazing. :) You?

I slipped on sandals, walked out of my room, and splashed some water on my face in the bathroom. The door to Mom and Dad's room was still closed.

Time to see the damage in the light of day. I'd snuck in through my bedroom window the night before.

With trepidation, I stepped into the kitchen and flicked on the switch. The shards of glass on the floor glinted like a million fallen pieces of a broken disco ball. Almost every pot and pan we owned lay across the floor from the kitchen to the living room. Previously sorted mail littered the ground like poorly made confetti.

My phone vibrated with a new message.

Andrew: You know when reality's better than your dreams and you don't want to fall asleep? My night was kind of like that.

My heart wrenched, scattered like the once-clean contents of our home.

Me: Last night was amazing. Thank you.

I set my phone on the counter and started cleaning up. Last night with Andrew had been the dream. This was my reality.

I could barely keep my eyes open in class. Andrew's kiss and my parents' fight had thrown me into this weird limbo between wishing for love and dreading where it could lead. It didn't help that Kellum kept sending me these painfully attractive smiles throughout A&P and weights.

Why did I feel like I was cheating? That was ridiculous, right? Kellum had asked me on a date, and Andrew, well, Andrew had bought me a cherry slushy then kissed me until the red on my lips had rubbed off on his. But Kellum had stood up to Shelby for me, so that had to mean something. But what?

Every day that week, Kellum sat with me at lunch, which meant Evan and the rest of the weights class sat with me at lunch. Andrew and I texted in the evenings, about school and life, never touching on what our kiss meant or what we were. I just knew I liked talking to him.

By Friday, my nerves strummed tightly in my chest with Kellum sitting next to me at lunch. I had less than twenty-four hours until my date with him and still no idea what I really wanted.

Shelby reached our table and practically slammed her tray down. Her silverware clattered off, and her Jell-O wobbled dangerously.

Rachel gave me a look. "Everything okay, Shel?"

Shelby picked up her fork and stabbed at her food. "You guys ready for the ACT? Because I am." She shoved a bite in her mouth. "Oh, and my Dad has my keys until I get a scholarship or apply for ten." Shelby pierced her Jell-O, slicing it in half. "So. Kellum, will you pick me up on your way into the test tomorrow?"

Rachel looked confused. "Aren't your parents paying for you to go to college?"

Shelby mimicked her dad's voice, "'There's no point in paying the whole bill if there are scholarships sitting out there for the taking. Just because we have the money doesn't mean we need to spend it.' Two more points on my ACT and I'll get way more scholarships anyway. It's stupid."

God forbid she actually had to write an essay or two to pay for her college education or go a week without her precious little hybrid car.

"Kellum," Shelby said, harsher this time. "Will you take me?"

Why did she think she had a claim on him just because he had to drive by her house on the way to school?

Kellum shook his head. "Sorry, I can't."

Shelby snorted. "What? Hot date?"

Zack met my eyes and winked. "Yeah, Kell, you have a hot date?"

I waited for the excuse. For Kellum to say he

couldn't because of a family thing or because he'd decided to skip.

"Yeah," Kellum said. "Actually, I do."

All the color drained from Shelby's face until she looked almost green.

Rachel's eyes lit up. "What? Who?"

Kellum bumped my shoulder.

And everyone went crazy.

"Wait. What?"

"Go Hoffner."

"No way!"

"You two will be so cute together!"

"What are you guys doing?"

Then Shelby. She stared straight at Kellum and glared. "You've got to be kidding me."

Kellum's brows knitted together. "What's that supposed to mean?"

The table fell silent, looking between Shelby, whose mouth gaped open and closed, and Kellum, whose warm chocolate eyes had fired to stone.

Shelby composed herself and rolled her eyes. "I mean, what is it? Are you taking her to Goodwill to buy bigger clothes or something?"

My jaw dropped. I hated confrontation, would usually let her walk all over me, but I was done. I was done dealing with Shelby and the crap she slung at me any chance she got. And I was done putting up with people talking about me like I wasn't there.

"You know what?" I snapped. "This is absolute bull—"

Kellum put a hand on my forearm and met my eyes. "I've got this."

Then he turned to Shelby. "This is absolute bullshit."

Zack snorted milk and lifted a napkin to his nose. "You got it," he said through a coughing fit.

Kellum looked from Zack back to Shelby again. "Seriously. This is enough. You've been talking crap about Skye ever since she got that stupid liberal—"

"Libero," Rachel corrected.

"—libero position, and I'm tired of it. You've been hell on her, and she's done nothing but take it. From now on, if you have a problem with Skye, you take it to me." His mouth stayed in a hard line, and everyone stared at him, shocked.

My eyes burned, and in seconds the dam overflowed, sending streams of tears down my cheeks.

I wiped at my eyes, got up, and went to the bathroom as fast as I could. I couldn't break down in front of Kellum, much less Shelby.

I locked myself in a stall and sat down. There, in the empty bathroom, my shoulders shook, my throat burned, and sobs wracked my chest. I knew I was being excessive, but I couldn't stop.

I felt...humiliated, justified, scared. No one had so publicly stood up for me and acknowledged what Shelby'd done. Not my so-called best friends, not my coach, no one. But I was so pathetic I'd never handled it myself. And here, Kellum, a guy I'd crushed on for years but who'd never really noticed me, was telling Shelby to "go through" him?

The bathroom door opened. "Skye?"

It was Rachel.

I stuffed my fist in my mouth and forced myself to breathe through my nose.

Her feet moved next to my stall, and she eyed me through the crack. "You okay?"

I sucked in another breath and moved my hand. "I don't know."

She leaned her head against the stall. "What Shelby said was totally uncalled for."

Tell me something I don't know.

Quiet fell between us.

"She just found out she didn't make the team at Upton," Rachel said. "Her dad was really mad at her about it."

I knew how much it hurt to have your dreams broken. The difference was that her dad would come around. Her parents would pay for her college. She would enjoy the four years and go on to get a great job, debt free, and start a life on her own, knowing she had the love and support of her family. She'd never know how much that was worth.

"So," Rachel said. "You and Kellum."

The words sounded strange in my ears. "Me and Kellum haven't even had our first date yet."

"Yeah, but you guys are gonna be so cute together." She paused. "What would your 'ship name be? Skyeum? Kellye? Wattner?"

Despite myself, I let out a shaky laugh. "Sttoooppp."

She laughed too. "Think you can come out?"

I balled up some of the .25-ply toilet paper schools always had and wiped at my eyes. "Yeah. Give me a second."

That evening, I went straight to my room. I didn't want to pretend I didn't hate Mom for staying. If Dad came home, I didn't want to have to face him and pretend like I didn't hate everything he'd done to our house, everything he'd said to Mom, the night before.

But he had been right about one thing. I wanted to leave as soon as I could.

I sat down at my desk and got out my calculus

homework. Nothing like solvable problems to distract me from the impossible ones in my own life.

My phone vibrated on my desk, and I picked it up.

Kellum: Hey, u ok? Never saw u after lunch.

My heart beat sideways. Kellum was checking up on me?

Me: Better now. Thanks for everything.

Kellum: Excited for tomorrow. :)

Kellum: Meet me at the school at 6.

Kellum: Don't worry about breakfast.

Me: See you then.

Kellum: Oh, and bring a swimsuit. ;)

And all of a sudden, I was my older sister in fourth grade, getting ready for a pool party and freaking out because I knew I didn't look good in my swimsuit.

My phone vibrated again.

Andrew: Hey, is it okay if I call you?

I smiled at the screen, my panic subsiding only slightly.

Me: I'll call you. Give me a sec.

I shrugged on a jacket and went to the living room. Mom was laying on the couch, a glass of wine on the floor beside her and a blanket up to her chin.

"I'm going on a walk."

Her eyes trailed up and down my outfit. "Wear gloves."

I hardly needed them—it had to be sixty degrees outside, but I didn't want to argue. "Sure." I grabbed a pair out of the closet, tucked them in my pocket, and went outside.

When I'd made it at least a hundred yards from the house, I dialed Andrew's number.

"Hello?" he asked.

I imagined the way his lips would form around the word and land in a smile. It brought a smile to my own lips and the phantom of cherry flavoring on my tongue.

"Hey," I said.

A cool breeze swept around me, and I angled the phone so he wouldn't hear too much static from the wind.

"What's up?" he asked.

I turned around the corner and started down the road where the pavement turned to gravel. "Getting ready for the ACT tomorrow. You?"

"Same." He sighed. "I have to miss a debate meet, though. Kinda stinks."

"Our coach basically made us take it."

He laughed, and the sound warmed me in a way the gloves never could. "Seriously?"

I smiled. "Yeah. But only because he's also our guidance counselor."

"How was your week?"

At the sinking feeling in my stomach, I switched the phone to my other ear. "It could have been better."

Concern practically dripped from his voice. "Oh no, is everything okay?"

I hesitated. I could lie, say "sure," and move on. Pretend I was this girl who could just kiss a guy and see where it led. Like I wasn't terrified of getting too close to anyone who could trap me in the kind of life my parents had. But wasn't lying what got my parents into their situation? They'd been lying to themselves for so many years that chaos seemed normal.

"Actually," I said, "not really. My parents..."

He waited.

"Well, they fight. A lot. And my dad. He throws things when he's mad."

"Skye." Andrew's voice was soft, gentle. "I'm so sorry."

And just like that, I found myself telling him everything. About my mom and how she put up with Dad's temper and him coming and going all hours of the night. How I needed my sister, the only person who actually got what I was going through, but didn't even have her number. And I admitted how much I desperately wanted to leave, to make something of myself so I never needed to live in a house with an old air conditioner, a man who didn't care, and clothes that never came straight off the rack.

And it was surprisingly easy to tell him. He listened, sympathized when he needed to, cracked a joke when I got too low, and, most importantly, he let me dream about the kind of life I could have when all of this was behind me.

"You have everything you need, Skye," he said. "You have a drive people with unimaginable amounts of money couldn't even dream of. You have this awesome ability to see things how they really are, and at the same time, you see how they should be. Everything that's happened to you wasn't your choice, but you're choosing to make something of yourself. People who've been through hell always do great things because they know how bad it can get, and they'll do anything to stop someone else from going through the same suffering."

And then he said the thing I needed to hear the most: "You're not going to end up like your parents."

I'd do anything to make sure he was right.

CHAPTER SEVENTEEN

I WOKE up at five and spent as much time on my hair and makeup as I would for prom. I used a straightener to put soft waves into my hair and brought out my eyes with neutral eyeshadow, eyeliner, and mascara. Even my lips shined with a light coat of shimmery gloss. My clothes weren't fancy or new, but they hugged my extra curves, and I hoped that would be good enough.

I stuffed my backpack with everything I'd need for the ACT—a calculator, plenty of No. 2 pencils, and an eraser—and added everything else. My swimming suit, a towel, and things to fix my hair and makeup before I got home.

Mom and Dad were still sleeping and thought I would be going to a debate meet. Since they didn't ever check up on meets I actually went to, it was a pretty safe bet I could get home around seven or eight and they'd be none the wiser.

On the drive to school, I listened to music, but Andrew's words still played through my mind.

He was right. I wasn't going to end up like my parents. I could create the kind of life I wanted, and I knew I would put in the work to do it. Starting by having an amazing day.

I was about to go on a date with my biggest crush. McClellan's homecoming king. A guy with a thousand-watt smile who had stood up for me without ever being asked.

Kellum's car idled in the school parking lot, a small stream of exhaust coming out the tailpipe, and I parked my pickup next to his. I grabbed my bag from the back and climbed into Kellum's vehicle.

"Good morning." He handed me a disposable mug and a burrito wrapped in foil. Both warmed my hands. "You like coffee, right?" he asked.

I nodded.

"Good." He grinned.

I grinned back. "Thanks."

And we were both grinning at each other like the dummies we were, about to sneak off to take a test and then wear swimsuits in February for whatever harebrained reason.

It was way too early for me to even try guessing.

He looked back at his steering wheel and put the car in gear. "Better get on the road."

We pulled out of the parking lot, out of town, and onto the highway. The tip of the sun barely peeked over the horizon ahead of us, giving way to pink-orange clouds and golden beams of light.

Kellum reached up and pulled a pair of sunglasses out of a compartment near the overhead lights. Wearing the dark, square shades with the sun hitting his face, he looked better than a model. Better than a dream. I could have watched the light trace paths over his lips all day.

He glanced over at me, and when he caught me staring, his mouth formed a slow smile. "What?"

I shook my head, a smile touching my own lips. "Nothing."

"Sure."

I peeled back the foil around my burrito and took a bite. The cheese had melted perfectly, and the blend of eggs, sausage, and onions flooded my mouth. "This is so good."

He smiled. "You think?"

I nodded. "Tell your mom thanks."

He acted offended. "I made them!"

Now I was shocked. I glanced at the burrito in my hand. "Seriously?"

"Seriously."

I golf clapped. "Nicely done."

He laughed. "The secret's in the cheese. After you put it in foil, you let it warm in the oven so it's all melty."

That piece of information got stored somewhere in my brain between calculus formulas and the exact shape of Kellum's left dimple.

Silence hung between us as I ate my burrito and sipped at my coffee. He switched the radio on, and something from the Top 40 played over the speakers. The music was just a little too loud for me, but I tried not to mind.

I finished my food and nursed my coffee. What should I say? Were we really going to ride the entire way to Austin without talking?

"So," I said.

He nudged the volume down. "So."

I breathed a little sigh out my nose, and he laughed.

What did he and Saffron talk about on dates? Was talking even on the agenda for them?

Ugh. I hated myself for thinking that.

"You're not even worried, are you?" he asked.

"About the test?" No. About the date? Definitely.

He nodded.

"I did alright last time. I need to score as high as I can, though. You?"

His shoulders lifted. "I mean, I got a twenty last time. I don't think even a couple of points either way would matter much."

"I get that." But I couldn't afford to think that way. Literally. "Did you decide which college you're going to?"

He shrugged. "I got into a couple schools. I'll probably go to Blackburn. Play some ball."

"Football?"

He shook his head. "Basketball. I might sit the bench, but I'll get books and tuition paid for."

It didn't sound like a bad setup, honestly. "You and Zack could be roomies."

"That's the plan. At least I'd know what I was getting myself into."

The fact that he only had three months, give or take, until he could graduate high school and leave for college had my stomach burning with jealousy. I didn't feel like I could make it even half that long.

"What about you? You know what you want to

do with your life?" He said it like it was a joke, and I guessed, considering the number of freshmen who changed their majors right away, it kind of was.

"I don't know yet. Maybe English."

"Starving artist?"

I barked out a laugh. I'd been financially starving long enough. I didn't need to do that any longer. "No way. Maybe marketing or counseling or social work. I really don't know. How did you know what you want to do?"

"I don't," he said. "I'm going into business so I can do anything."

"Except brain surgery."

He laughed.

"And phlebotomy."

"Not medically, anyway."

I laughed that time. "Or what if you wanted to fly a plane?"

"No way."

"What do you mean?" The thought of flying so high overhead that McClellan was just a speck on the ground seemed amazing to me.

"I'm terrified of flying. Honestly, I'd rather drive fifteen hours than get on a plane."

My jaw dropped. "Seriously?"

"Yep. But, I mean, why would I?"

"Why would you what?"

"Why would I want to go anywhere else? My family's here. If I want to see a beach, I can drive to Galveston. If I want mountains, I can cross the border and go to Ruidoso. Sand dunes? We've got those too, and rivers and lakes and woods." He shrugged. "I've got everything I need."

I wanted to believe him, I really did. I wanted to buy into this idea of Texas being great and not needing to leave, but I couldn't. There was so much of the world to see—foreign foods to taste, different mountains to climb, all kinds of people to meet.

And then it hit me. We were totally different, came from two totally different places, even though we lived less than five miles apart.

Kellum set up the GPS to take us to Upton, and for the rest of the trip, I navigated. We arrived a few minutes early—a first for Kellum—and got all set up to take our exams.

For the next four mind-numbing hours, we took test after test with hundreds of other students. My wrist ached from filling in bubbles, my eyes drooped from getting up so early, and my head hurt from working so many problems.

Finally, finally, they picked up the last of our tests, and I met Kellum by the water fountains.

"Ready to go?" he asked.

"I'm ready to sleep for a week."

He laughed. "I've got something else planned first."

I gulped. My swimsuit. "Where are we going?"

He took my hand and wound his fingers through mine. Despite my doubts, my stomach swooped, and electricity shot up my arm.

"Let's go," he said, but I was already following him.

We drove across town, and Kellum parked in front of a massive indoor waterpark.

"No way."

He nodded. "Sounds fun, right?"

The hopeful tone in his voice softened the edges of my ragged nerves. "Definitely. I'll just have to be careful with my knee."

He smiled. "Of course. I'll carry you if I need to."

The thought of resting snugly in Kellum's arms warmed parts of me I didn't even know existed. What would it feel like to curl up against his muscled chest? To have a guy actually be able to lift me?

"Promise?" I asked, trying to be coy, but probably sounding dumb.

"Pinky swear."

He held his little finger out, and I wrapped mine around his. Heat flowed from our connection up my arm and pooled in my stomach. How was this happening?

I grabbed my backpack from the backseat, and he picked up a stuffed drawstring bag. We walked together to the front window, and Kellum paid my way in. Nineteen dollars and twenty-eight cents, to be exact.

I thanked him about a million and one times before he told me to go change and meet him by the pool.

In the locker room, I slipped into my one-piece suit. It was simple—black with white straps, but at least it hid some of the new cushion that had taken up residence on my stomach. My thighs still rubbed together, and I tugged down on the bottom of the suit so it laid flat over my bottom.

As I ran my hands over the fabric, I felt little balls of worn thread, proving how old it was.

What I was I doing here? Saffron wouldn't be wearing an old one-piece on a date with Kellum. Surely, she'd have a cute bikini and at least rubbed on some fake tanner over her flat stomach and toned thighs to hide her tan lines.

But Kellum had asked me, I reminded myself. Not her.

So, I lifted my chin, sucked in my gut, and stepped out of the locker room.

I saw Kellum before he saw me, and man, did he look good. His shorts hung low enough on his hips to see the lines of his hipbones and the V shape his broad shoulders made. His back muscles stood out, even in his relaxed stance.

This guy had asked me out? Me?

He turned, and when he caught my eye, he smiled like he didn't care about my ratty suit or the fact that my hair was already frizzing from the humidity lifting from the pool. "Hey there."

I smiled. "Hey yourself."

His hand easily found mine, and my stomach reacted the way it had before. I hoped he didn't notice the goosebumps rising on my arms.

"What first?" he asked.

I scanned the pool, from the monkey bars hanging over the water, to the giant slides that wound around each other over the lazy river couples were floating on. "Slides?" That seemed like a safe answer.

He grinned and scanned the towers. "Which one do you want?"

There were four. One that basically dropped straight down, one that was a little less steep and the two that curled around like snaking tunnels. I pointed at the curving one on the far right.

He inclined his head toward the steep slide. "I've got that one."

I grinned. "Showoff."

A laugh swelled from his chest and fell off his lips. "I have to be when there's a pretty girl around."

My tongue got heavy, and I couldn't speak over all the blood rushing to my head. Me? Pretty?

"Come on," he said and tugged my hand so I'd follow him toward the stairs.

He tried to get me to go up first, but no way was I putting my behind on display walking up a hundred stairs. He finally agreed to lead and started up. I followed. Stairsteps were one of my rehab exercises after all.

We finally made it to the top, and I noticed Kellum's face grow pale.

"Too high?" I asked.

He jerked his head left and right and forced a smile. "No way."

I playfully narrowed my eyes at him. "Uh huh."

His arms went across his chest in a ripple of golden skin and muscles. "I am not scared."

"Uh huh." I went to the rail and leaned over to watch all the people swimming and walking around below. "Come check it out."

Kellum stood a foot back from the rail and peeked over. "Yeah, cool."

I put my back to the rail. "Scaredy cat."

"'Scaredy cat'?"

I jutted my chin out. "You heard me."

His eyes danced with the challenge. He steeled his jaw, and slowly, measuredly stepped to the edge, leaning over until his chest rested on the railing. Then he turned his head to me, and even though he looked green, he smiled. "See?"

I laughed. "Okay, okay, you're not a scaredy cat. But we'll see how you do about the slide."

His Adam's apple bobbed. "You'll see."

The line thinned until both of us waited in front of our prospective slides. The lifeguard gave me the go-ahead. His did too. He glanced at me, nodded.

I used the handle to launch myself down the slide and got lost in the darkness of the tube, the rush of water, and the smell of chlorine.

The slide launched me into a shallow pool, and I stayed below the water for a second, enjoying the silence, the cover from Kellum's eyes, and then I surfaced, breathing in fully.

Kellum was already waiting at the steps, his slide having sent him down faster.

"Was that you I heard screaming?" I asked.

Was it just me or did his cheeks get red?

I laughed. "Kidding, Kellum! Kidding."

He chuckled. "I didn't scream, but I got a massive wedgie. Like of Victoria's Secret proportions."

An image of Kellum in a lacy thong popped into my mind, and I laughed. "I'm glad you survived that."

"Me too."

I stepped out of the pool, and we both walked away from the slides. We'd save the wedgies for another time.

"Wave pool?" he asked.

I nodded. "Sure."

I'd only been in a wave pool once when I was younger, and I never really got it. Usually, it was just a bunch of people standing around and waiting for the water to move. This time was no different, except I had Kellum next to me.

A big wave crashed into us, and I bumped into him. The skin of his chest slid over my arm, and that warm feeling spread across my stomach again. His eyes, framed by wet eyelashes, held mine, and I got lost in their chocolate depths, wondering why no one else had brown eyes like his. They were so special.

He blinked, breaking his hold on me, and I looked away.

"The waves stopped," he said.

Oh. He was right. The water had flattened out.

"Lazy river?" he asked.

I nodded. Maybe a change of setting would calm all these butterflies crash testing their wings in my stomach.

I followed him out of the wave pool and he walked to a massive pile of circular pool floats. He picked one up and handed it to me then grabbed his own.

We stepped into the river, and the current immediately caught my legs. I used my right leg to hop myself into the float and adjusted myself in the ring until I could lean back comfortably.

Kellum paddled until his raft touched mine, and he grabbed onto one of the handles. "Here, give me your feet."

"My feet?"

He nodded, and I shifted until I could rest my legs in his lap. Thankfully, I'd shaved the night before.

His hand moved to my calves, and he ran it easily up and down my leg. "This is nice."

I smiled at him, at this situation I never dreamed I'd find myself in. "Yeah, it is."

The river took us farther away from the commotion of the pool. The lack of sound seemed loud to me, especially with Kellum's hands on my legs.

He traced a finger up my shin and gently touched the scar from my surgery.

It felt strange, like the skin didn't have any nerves but the muscles below it did.

"How are you doing with everything?" he asked.

I shrugged. "It hasn't been easy."

"I bet."

"Thanks for not saying anything about when I woke up."

A smile cracked his somber expression. "I mean, I needed to keep a girl like that to myself."

I lightly kicked his stomach with my foot, and he laughed.

We left it at that, and Kellum didn't press further. We floated around the lazy river, his soft touch sending tingles up every single one of my nerves.

We hung out at the water park until three. It was

only the middle of the afternoon, but I knew my clock was striking midnight.

Kellum got me lunch at a drive-through, and we started the trip home. After getting up early and being at the water park, I felt so sleepy.

He told me to nap, and I leaned my head against the seat, falling asleep with his fingers intertwined in mine.

"Skye," he whispered. "Skye."

I blinked my eyes open, seeing the school in front of me.

"We're back."

I wiped at my face in case I'd drooled and stifled a yawn.

Kellum smiled at me like it was the cutest thing he'd seen.

I smiled back at him, clueless. What did I say now? How could I ever thank him? Tell him how much this whole day had meant to me?

"Thanks for coming out with me," he said.

My lips lifted back into an easy, sleepy smile. "Thank you so much. Everything was...perfect."

"Well." He tilted his head to the side. "Not quite."

I frowned. Had I done something wrong.

His hand lifted, and the backs of his fingers

traced a pattern from my temple to my cheek. Slowly, he leaned in, closer, closer, until I smelled his gum, and then chlorine, and then his lips landed on mine. Light burst behind my closed eyelids, and I lost a grip on everything except the guy kissing me like we had nowhere else to be.

Too soon, it was over.

"Okay," he said. "Now it was perfect."

Stunned at his lips, at the hazy way he was looking at me, I nodded.

He reached into the backseat and handed me my bag. "See you Monday."

"See you Monday," I said and got out of the car.

CHAPTER EIGHTEEN

~Prom~

Juniors meet in the FAQS room during lunch for a prom meeting! We have two months to plan!

Your Class Sponsors,

Taylor and Earl Gormsley

I pulled the note off of my locker, staring at it. Prom was only two months away? I hadn't even bought a dress. Or found a date. Oh my gosh, a date. My heart swung from vein to vein like a confused monkey. What was I going to do?

The meeting left me plenty of time to think about it. Most of the girls in my class, Kylie at the forefront, argued about what the prom theme should be while the guys joked around with each other and contributed absolutely nothing. I picked at my food, still sorting my thoughts. How had I, Miss Almost-Never-Been-Kissed, actually kissed two guys within a week of each other?

Kellum would be the obvious option for me to take to prom. I mean, he was here, nearby, popular, kind, and he would look incredible in my prom pictures. But Andrew... I couldn't get him off my mind. Rhett had said to choose someone who looked like my future. How could I choose Kellum when all he saw in his future was Texas?

I stayed after school to practice policy debate with Reese, but I called Andrew on the way home.

"Hey, what are you up to?"

"Just studying," he said. "You?"

"Reese—my policy debate partner—is running me through the ringer. He gave me like a million articles to read through on GMOs and conventional versus organic farming." I glared at the stack of papers at least two inches thick sitting in my passenger seat. "I never realized how much work debate takes."

"He sounds like a good partner," Andrew said. "I need to catch up on some of my research too."

"At least I'm not alone."

"Of course not." His voice softened. "Have things eased up at home?"

I shrugged even though he couldn't see me. "I mean, define 'eased up.'"

"Your dad came back?"

I sighed. "Yep. And everyone's back to acting like nothing happened."

"Ugh. That sucks."

"Uh huh," I said. "And I heard my parents doing...it the night he got back." I shuddered. "That's not great under normal circumstances, but it was so gross."

"Naaaaasty," Andrew said.

"I know." My lips pulled down, and my nose scrunched like I'd smelled a skunk. Wait. That was an actual skunk. "Ugh. Anyway, changing the subject."

"Thank God."

I laughed.

"So," he said.

"Anything new?" I asked.

"Well, I was actually wondering what you were doing after your debate meet this Saturday?"

What did I ever do on a Saturday night? Stay home and try to avoid my parents. "Nothing really. Why do you ask?"

"I thought maybe you'd like to catch a movie if one's playing there around eight? I could pick you up."

My lips spread faster than butter on a hot pan. "Like a date?"

I barely heard the soft chuckle on his end of the phone. "Exactly like that."

I saw my house ahead, and I slowed down. "I'd love to," I said before thinking. "Talk to you later?"

"Definitely. See ya."

The call ended, and I sat my phone down in my lap.

Crap.

I'd just agreed to a date with Andrew, in my hometown. What had I been thinking? There were a million ways it could go wrong, but three jumped out at me: my parents and Kellum. Kellum was going to be out of town for the weekend visiting family in Galveston, so we didn't have a date planned or anything. But what would my parents say about me going to the movies with this guy? But I had to ask them, especially if the date was in McClellan where everyone knew everyone's business.

I parked in the driveway and leaned my head back. Liz would have had some advice. She dated guys in high school—that was half the reason she and our parents argued so much. And I knew she used to sneak out our window some nights. I wasn't gutsy enough to do that.

I picked my phone up and scrolled down to the number that wasn't hers anymore. I called it anyway.

It rang a few times, and eventually a guy answered.

"Is Liz there?" I tried, already knowing the answer.

"Look," the guy sounded grumpy, "I don't know a Liz. She doesn't live here. And if you get a hold of her, tell her to tell everyone else she changed her number." Click.

I sighed. There was only one thing I could do: ask my parents before I lost the nerve.

I sucked in a deep breath, grabbed my backpack and research papers, and walked inside. Mom and Dad sat watching some show about antiques on the TV. They were showing a dresser that looked more beat up than mine and saying it was worth three thousand dollars. Yeah right.

I set my backpack on the floor and papers on the counter, and Mom looked back at me. "Put those away."

I kept my groan to myself and brought my stuff to my room. I didn't need to make them mad before asking to go on my first real date since Dad lost it with James.

I walked back out of my room and stood near the TV. "Mom? Dad? Can I talk to you guys for a sec?"

They eyed me wearily.

Dad took a drink. "What's up, squirt?"

He usually only called me that when he was in a good mood. That was a great sign.

"Well." I wrung my hands behind my back. First rule of dealing with the parents: show no signs of weakness. "One of my friends asked me on a date Saturday—to the movies—and I was wondering if I could get your permission?"

Mom's face blanched, and they looked at each other.

"I am a junior," I jumped in. "And it will just be to the movies and back. All of my grades are A's and above."

Dad scrubbed his chin. "Who is it?"

"He's a guy from Woodman. Andrew Brindon," I added, even though they wouldn't know him.

Mom jumped in, "How'd you meet him?"

"Debate."

"What?" Dad asked.

"The thing I do on Saturdays—arguments and speeches and stuff."

"Oh." He nodded. "I don't know if I want you going out with someone I don't know."

That was funny, because I didn't want to go out with anyone he did know. "He said he could come pick me up." It was a last resort, but I'd rather Andrew see where I live than never see me at all.

Mom and Dad looked at each other.

"Fine," Dad said, "but if I don't like him, I'm sending him straight home."

I wanted to argue, to say if they didn't trust my choice in men it said more about them as parents and what they thought of me. But if this thing with Andrew was going somewhere, everything had to be above board. At least until I knew where it was going.

"Now, help your mom cook supper," Dad said. "I'm hungry."

CHAPTER NINETEEN

FOR THE REST of the week, my life fell into a pattern I couldn't really complain about. During A&P, Kellum and Zack started sitting beside me in the back row, and between the two of them I had to fight to get any decent notes.

At lunch, the weights class sat together, and after school, Reese and I met at a diner to study. He always ordered me a coffee, saying, "If we have any hopes of placing at state, you need to be alert. And we need all the help we can get."

I couldn't really disagree. Coming up with solid arguments off the top of my head had never been my strong suit.

Afterwards, Andrew and I would talk on the phone on my way home from school, and I'd text both him and Kellum in the evening, being especially careful not to send my replies to the wrong person.

Sometimes I felt guilty, but going off of my limited knowledge—which I'd basically gained from watching *Sex and the City* and *Pretty Little Liars* when my parents were out of the house—it wasn't cheating. Not until we had the girlfriend/boyfriend talk. Still, I had to get this figured out. And soon.

I felt like such an idiot that I couldn't choose. Honestly, me even a month ago would have slapped me across the face for not immediately choosing Kellum and screamed, "SNAP OUT OF IT. WHO ARE YOU, AND WHAT HAVE YOU DONE WITH SKYE?"

But things were different now. I couldn't get Rhett's stupid (but maybe not-so-stupid?) advice out of my head.

Before I knew it, it was Saturday night, and I was changing out of the business professional clothes I'd worn for debate and into the jeans and solid black sweater I'd wear for my first official date with Andrew.

He texted me to say he was leaving Woodman, and I flew around the house, cleaning things that were dirty, dusting pictures, and making sure every last whiskey and wine bottle were out of sight.

Mom noticed me but didn't say anything. Dad was oblivious.

About five minutes before Andrew arrived, I had no idea what to do. I didn't want to sit in the window like a little abandoned puppy, but I also wanted to answer the door before Mom or Dad could. I settled for sitting on the couch by Mom, ears perked for the sound of his engine.

Eventually, I heard rocks crackle in the driveway and an engine stop.

Adrenaline flooded my chest. I hadn't even been this nervous the first time we met up. For whatever reason, this felt more serious. More real than an unplanned rendezvous. I stood straight out of the couch and headed for the door.

"Is that him?" Dad asked.

I nodded.

"Look sharp," Mom said with a coy smile at Dad.

She was enjoying this?

I waited with my hand near the knob until a few quick knocks sounded on the door. Andrew.

I took a deep breath and waited a few seconds so it wouldn't be so obvious, then opened the door to see Andrew holding a bouquet of multi-colored carnations. My heart melted at his sweet smile and the brightness of his eyes.

He'd dressed just like I'd coached him to. Simple and clean, in a pair of dark blue jeans, a white t-shirt, and an unbuttoned red and black flannel. No brand name clothes or fancy shoes.

He handed me the flowers. "These are for you."

I smiled and held them, trying to stay steady despite the rush in my stomach. "Thank you."

Dad's chair squeaked as he stood up, and his heavy footsteps fell toward us. He put his left hand on my shoulder and extended his right hand.

Andrew shook it, keeping his shoulders square.

"Dad," I said, "this is Andrew. Andrew, Dad."

"Nice to meet you, Mr. Hoffner," Andrew said.

Dad's cheeks lifted. He probably hadn't been called Mr. Hoffner in years, except by credit card companies. "Same to you."

Mom appeared next to Dad and wrapped her left arm around his waist so the three of us formed this odd, dysfunctional chain.

"This is my mom," I said.

Andrew nodded and shook her hand. "Pleasure, Mrs. Hoffner."

Okay, that was laying it on pretty thick, but Mom seemed appeased.

"Those are beautiful flowers," she said. "Let's put them in a vase, Skye."

I nodded, even though I wasn't sure we actually owned a vase.

Dad invited Andrew to sit in the living room with him, and I hurried to the kitchen with Mom, not wanting to miss a word passed between the two. She used a chair to reach one of the highest cabinets —the kind you abandon things in—and retrieved a dusty crystal vase.

Wordlessly, she rinsed it off and added water and sugar.

"Why are you putting sugar in it?" I asked.

"It's like plant food," she said and took the flowers from me. "You know, when I was your age, I used to get flowers too."

A shard of my heart broke loose. What did it say about my family that I hadn't seen flowers in our house for years? That Mom had to put her nice things on the highest shelf so they wouldn't get shattered.

I admired the purple, pink, orange, and blue-tipped carnations, loving the bright colors and wavy patterns of the flowers. I loved even more that they were mine.

Mom and I joined Andrew and Dad in the living room. The recliner didn't face toward the couch—it faced the TV—but Dad was twisted so he could talk to Andrew, who was mid explanation.

"—if you add lime and blended celery with your tomato juice, it gives your chili a richer flavor, especially if you're using a lot of beans," Andrew said.

Chili?

"Whatcha guys talking about?" I asked.

Dad lifted his eyebrows in an impressed expression I almost never saw him wear. "Andrew here said he and his parents travel over the summer for chili cookoffs."

A laugh fell through my lips. "What?"

Andrew nodded. "It's true. Mom has the best recipe. You guys will have to come to the fair in Woodman this summer to try it out."

Dad nodded. "Sounds like it."

Mom sat down on the couch opposite Andrew. "That would be great."

What? Were my parents seriously making a date with Andrew?

Dad looked over at me. "Are you gonna sit down?"

"Um, I think Andrew and I need to get on the road." Besides, sitting between my mom and my maybe-almost-not-quite boyfriend seemed like it would be awkward.

Dad looked at the box under the TV. "You've still got ten minutes before you need to leave."

I tried my best to smile. "What about snacks?"

He waved his hand. "Alright, go, go. Have fun."

"Curfew?" Mom asked.

Dad rubbed his chin. "Let's say half an hour after the movie gets out?"

Mom nodded. "And not a minute later."

"Yes, ma'am," Andrew said.

I picked up my purse. "See ya."

CHAPTER TWENTY

WE WALKED out to his car, and Andrew opened the door for me.

"What a gentleman," I teased.

He gave a little bow. "That's what a lady deserves, right?"

I rolled my eyes. "Uh huh."

"You in?" he asked.

I nodded, and he walked around to his side of the car.

"Really," I said. "My parents love you."

He backed out of the drive and tried acting nonchalant with a shrug, but his smile gave him away. "You think?"

"Oh please," I said. "My parents ate up all that 'yes ma'am,' 'Mr. Hoffner' stuff."

We started down the road, and he turned toward Main Street where the one movie theatre in town was.

He glanced over at me. "And what about you?"

"What about me?"

One corner of his mouth tipped up. "Did you eat it up?"

The thought of flowers and his bright eyes under short, wavy hair made my stomach twist. In a good way. "Maybe."

At the one streetlight in town, he slowed to a stop.

"That, and chili," I teased.

His smile spread. "Yeah, well, we are pretty good at making chili."

I watched him, his slightly pink cheeks, his lean hands holding the steering wheel, and smiled. I couldn't help myself.

He glanced over and caught me looking at him. "What?"

I smiled a little more but gazed at my lap. "Nothing. I just kinda like you."

"You're not too bad either."

We pulled up to the movie theatre, and I got out before he could grab my door. As we walked across the street, he hit the lock button on his key fob, and his car honked twice. That was nice. I always had to use my keys to unlock the door to my pickup.

There was a huge line inside—mostly parents with gaggles of little kids. The only movie playing that weekend was animated and rated G, but I'd take what I could get. Plus, it meant most people my age wouldn't be there, which didn't upset me one bit.

Andrew bought tickets, popcorn, and drinks for us, and we found seats near the back. The lights dimmed to black, and the screen lit up with a big green message.

"Hey," he said. "Did you know they're going to show us previews?"

I glanced from the screen to his face, feigning shock. "You're kidding."

He nodded seriously and pointed at the screen. "See? It's been approved." He lowered his voice. "For a general audience."

I covered my mouth. "Oh, how horrible."

He grinned. "I think we're good."

"Phew." I flicked imaginary sweat off my face. "Thank goodness."

A grin settled on his lips, and he looked at me, his expression unreadable.

"What?" I asked.

He shook his head slightly. "You're cute."

A small laugh started in my stomach and blew out my nose. "Ha."

"No, really." He brushed his thumb under my chin.

It left a trail of heat, and I tucked my cheek onto my shoulder. "You think?"

He nodded and dropped a kiss on my forehead. "Really."

Sitting with him, feeling his lips on my skin, seemed so comfortable, right. Like we'd been friends for years instead of months.

Another message crossed the screen about leaving phones on silent. Andrew reached into his pocket, retrieved his cell, and flicked his volume off. "You good?" he asked.

With a smile, I nodded.

We settled back into our seats, and Andrew left his open hand on the armrest between us. I watched it, the gentle curl of his fingers, and rested my hand in his until our fingers wound around each other and our palms touched. The pressure of his palm left a warm feeling that spread through my fingers and throughout my body.

For the rest of the movie, we sat like that, occasionally making jokes about something silly that happened onscreen or predicting what would happen next. I told Andrew all the guessing would ruin the ending, but he said the fun of a movie wasn't how it ended—it was the experience of watching it.

Afterward, we walked to his car and got in.

"9:35," he said. "Remember that."

I nodded. How could I forget? There was no way I was letting the drama that had unfolded with James happen with Andrew.

He put the car in reverse and pulled out.

"Where are we going?" I asked.

He looked over and smiled at me. "I don't know. Just driving."

We drove down Main, down the highway, and only stopped when we were on a dirt road, which didn't take too long around here.

He turned the car off and pulled the moon roof back. "I wanted to take you stargazing. Even if it was just for a couple minutes."

He leaned his seat all the way back, and I did the same. Through the glass, I caught sight of at least a hundred stars—probably more.

"It's fun to look at the sky," I said.

"Yeah, it is."

I caught him looking at me and rolled my eyes. "Laaaaaaaame."

He laughed. "Low hanging fruit, Skye. I had to!"

"No, no, no." I shook my head, laughing with him. "You can do better than that."

"You're right." He took my hand.

I rolled my head to the side on the headrest so I could watch him.

"Skye. You're...beautiful. And funny and smart and driven. I used to think that high school relationships were stupid. You know, statistics and divorce rates and drama and all of that. But, then I saw you. And I couldn't stop seeing you. It was like, no matter what I did, I couldn't stop looking at you, wondering what it would be like to be your friend. Wondering what it would be like to be something more."

My heart pounded with each of his words. They hit me right in the core, and I saved every single one of them so I could replay them in my mind on nights darker than this one.

"I've never met someone so determined and kind despite going through the challenges you have. You make me want to live in the moment and live in the future at the same time so I know everything I have to look forward to."

Breathless, I searched his eyes. His words had echoed Rhett's. Did he mean it?

"Skye." He covered my hand with both of his so I was surrounded by his touch. "I want to date you.

And I'm hoping you want to date me too. Exclusively."

My heart hammered in my chest, in my ears, in the tips of my fingers, in my skin under his hands. "You want me to be your girlfriend?"

He smiled one of his muted sunrise smiles and nodded. "Will you?"

For all the time I'd spent thinking about it, imagining this moment, I never imagined how easy it would be to say yes. "I'd love to."

His smile went from sunrise to full-on midday sun, and the brightness in him somehow transferred through the air, filling me up until I couldn't help smiling wide.

Still grinning, he moved closer and kissed me, and between kisses, he said, "That makes me so happy."

"Me too."

We kissed only a few minutes longer than we should have. And Andrew got me home, just in time for curfew.

Mom and Dad were both on the couch when I walked in the door. I fought my smile—if I looked too happy, they'd be suspicious. But it was hard to act normal when my heartstrings were strumming Andrew's name.

"How was it?" Mom asked.

I glanced at the flowers Andrew got me sitting on the island. "It was great. Thanks for letting me go."

Dad stood up. "Seems like a good kid."

Now I couldn't help my expression. "Yeah, I think so."

I said goodnight and went into my room. It wasn't until right before I closed my eyes to sleep that I realized the one problem with tonight: I had to tell Kellum.

CHAPTER TWENTY-ONE

I GOT to school on time Monday, dreading telling Kellum. I decided I'd wait until after he got out of track practice so he could have the evening to think about it at home—if he even cared. *Sex and the City* hadn't prepared me for breaking up with my dream guy. I'd practiced what I'd say at least a million times, and I tried reminding myself that we'd only been on one date, but I still felt nervous.

I sat down in my seat in A&P, but neither Zack nor Kellum were there yet. For Kellum, that wasn't too unusual—he seemed to perpetually run about ten minutes late—but Zack always showed up at least five minutes before the bell.

When Mrs. Valor set up her notes on the table in front of the board, they still weren't in.

"Before I start with the lesson," Mrs. Valor said, "are there any questions?"

She looked around the class, and no one raised their hands.

"I said," she raised her voice toward the door, "are there any questions?"

The door opened, and Zack walked in with a giant paper sign that read OUT OF ALL THE FISH IN THE SEA...

Then Kellum entered behind him, looking stunning in that dark green sweater I loved and holding a tank with a beta fish inside.

"Will you go to prom with me?" he asked.

Oh no. *No, no, no, no, no.*

My butt stayed planted in the chair, frozen, just like my moronic mouth and mind.

"Skye?"

My mouth gaped open and closed, just like that stupid blue fish, and if I didn't breathe, soon, I'd be the same color.

People were starting to whisper.

"Kellum?" I choked out. "Can we talk in the hallway?"

Zack's mouth dropped open. "You're not gonna say no, are you?"

Kellum glanced over at him. "It's cool. Yeah, let's go."

I stumbled out of my chair and followed Kellum into the hallway. My feet shook with each step.

I closed the door behind me, and Kellum turned to face me, still holding the tank. Now, I noticed the rocks inside spelled PROM?

I was going to hell for this.

"What's up?" he asked. His lips had formed that classic Kellum smile, but the tightness around his eyes gave his nerves away.

What could I tell him? If he would have asked me even a month ago—in front of Saffron no less—I would have thought I'd died and gone to heaven, like, sitting with God on his armchair with a bucket of ice cream kind of heaven.

But now? "Kellum, I'm sorry, but I can't go with you."

His shoulders drooped. "Are you going to be out of town or something?"

I wished. "No. Um, I... I have a boyfriend. It's new, but..." I let the sentence hang and watched as Kellum took it in.

"Seriously?"

My face scrunched. Was I really that undateable?

He adjusted the fish and ran his hand through his hair. "That came out wrong. I mean. I thought we had a nice time? Have you been dating another guy?"

Define dating. "Not really. We've been talking since I hurt my knee, and he asked me to be exclusive with him."

A deep breath lifted his shoulders, and he looked away.

"I did have a great time with you," I said. "The best time. But you want to stay in Texas, and I want to be...anywhere else."

He met my eyes. "That's what this is about? You know, you don't have to take everything so seriously. It's just high school. Things could change."

Ouch. So that meant he hadn't taken our date seriously, or me. "Yeah, Kellum, things could change, but I'm not going to change my mind. I'm not risking getting stuck in McClellan."

"Okay." His jaw muscle tensed, and he wouldn't meet my eyes. "Keep the fish." He shoved the tank into my hands, then turned and left.

I walked into A&P carrying the only proof I had that, out of all the fish in the sea, Kellum had wanted to go to prom with me.

CHAPTER TWENTY-TWO

BY WEIGHTS CLASS, everyone in the school had heard of Kellum's failed promposal and either stopped by my locker to look at the fish and suggest a name or express their shock I'd said no. It was the most visible I'd felt since the beginning of the year, and I hated it. I knew everyone was talking about me, making up rumors, thinking I was deranged.

Maybe I was.

Kellum didn't talk to me in weights, but the weights class did sit together at lunch. Kaiser, the idiot he was, brought it up again.

"So, who are you going to prom with, Skye?"

Kellum and I both glared at him.

He put his hands up. "What? Just asking."

Shelby looked way too pleased with everything.

"Skye probably doesn't have a date."

"What does that mean?" I asked.

She shrugged. "I mean, come on, it's not like you could do better than Kellum."

I raised my eyebrows, feeling insulted for both myself and Andrew. "Oh really?"

"Yeah. No offense, but the real question is why he ever asked you to prom in the first place."

Kellum stood up with his tray and stared down at her. "That's enough, Shelby."

She shrank back and directed her eyes at her own tray. I looked gratefully up at Kellum, but he was already walking to drop off his tray.

I stood up and followed him. "Hey, Kell."

He stopped, his back to me.

I caught up and tried to meet his eyes. Finally, he looked at me with those beautiful chocolate orbs.

"Thanks," I said. "For everything."

For a second, his features softened. "No problem."

After school, I ran into a problem. Fish transportation.

I had to drive to the diner to study with Reese,

and I didn't want to kill it. I settled on buckling it into the passenger seat and driving about fifteen miles below the speed limit the whole way there.

I brought it inside the diner with me, and Reese looked up from his seat at it.

"You didn't flush that thing?" he asked.

I rolled my eyes. "Good to see you too."

He sat his phone down. "I suppose. So, who's the guy?"

I gave him a quizzical look.

"Come on, Hoffner. You're too smart to act dumb. Who are you dating?"

I raised my eyebrows and sat down. "I thought you didn't get involved in school drama."

With his nose in the air, he straightened his blazer. "Not until it affects my chances at state. And you're my partner, so..."

I sighed. "Remember that guy at my first meet?"

Reese looked horrified. "The one hanging out the bus window?"

"Don't look at me like that," I said, on a roll. Usually I avoided confrontation, but if I could say no to prom with Kellum, I could do anything.

A pleased expression crossed Reese's face. "Nicely done, Hoffner. Someone needed to tell Watts no."

Reese's praise made me feel oddly proud, and for the first time that day, I didn't feel so guilty.

Reese snapped his fingers at the waitress. "Coffee for her." He pointed at me. "Actually, make it two."

We studied hard and practiced harder for two and half hours. But after our conversation about prom, no matter how brief, I was starting to see him as more than a debate partner. Almost as a friend.

I left the diner with my fish and buckled it into the passenger seat again. On the road, I dialed Andrew.

As it rang, I glanced at the fish. "What should I name you?"

"What?" Andrew answered. He must have heard me.

"Nothing. What's up?"

"Oh, just homework. You?"

"On my way home from debate practice."

"Awesome. How are you feeling?"

I took a quick assessment of my body. "Fine. Why?"

A low chuckle reached my ear. "I mean about us? You know, being boyfriend and girlfriend?"

"Ah. That. Good." I smiled wide, even though no one could see me. "Great, actually."

"Me too." I heard the happiness in his voice. "So, when can I take you out next?"

"Well. I mean, we'll probably see each other before then, but what are you doing the last Saturday in April?"

"Hmm," he drew it out like he was flipping through a calendar. "Going to prom."

I sat further up in my seat. "What? How did you know I was going to ask you?"

"Huh?"

"I was going to ask you to my prom," I said, turning down a side road so I wouldn't have to go home yet.

"Oh no," he said. "Our proms are on the same day."

"Well, shoot."

"What?"

I just turned down the most popular guy at McClellan because I was dating someone else, and now I'd have to go to prom alone. "Nothing. I was just planning on asking you."

He was quiet for a second. "I wish we could go together."

"We still could?"

"I would love to go with you," he said, "see how beautiful you'd look in a prom dress. But I'm on student council, so I have to be at my prom, and I'm not asking you to miss yours."

It made sense. Logically. So why did my heart hurt?

"You could take a friend?" he suggested.

"Maybe." If I had one. "Well, I've got to go do some homework, so I'll talk to you later... Bye."

I tossed my phone in the passenger seat by the fish and went around the block another time before going home.

When I pulled up, I walked to the door and knocked with my foot so I wouldn't have to put the tank down.

Mom came to the door and gave me a quizzical look. "What's with the fish?"

I walked inside. "It's a long story."

She closed the door behind me. "Condensed version."

I looked down at the gravel PROM? That was starting to look more disheveled. "Long story short, I got asked to prom, said no because I'm dating Andrew, and now I have a fish."

She nodded slowly. "Well, you're going to have to take care of it."

"Yep," I said, and I walked to my room.

I set the fish on Liz's old dresser and flopped

down on my bed. I needed to tell someone about all the craziness that had ensued, but I couldn't exactly share the fish story with Andrew.

Me: I'm an idiot.

Anika: ????

I texted her the full version of Kellum's promposal and ended with Andrew not being able to go.

Anika: Whoa. You've been busy!

Me: LOL no kidding.

Anika: I can't believe you turned down Kellum.

Me: Me neither.

Me: Am I crazy?

Anika: No way. When you know, you know.

Me: Yeah. Just sucks to go to prom alone.

Anika: Can you sign me and Brandon in? Then you'll have 2 dates. :)

Me: You mean it?

Anika: Of course.

I smiled down at my phone. This felt nice. To have a friend and an actual boyfriend to talk to.

Anika: Well, I better go eat.

Me: See ya

Anika: Later :)

I set my phone on the bed beside me.

Now, to figure out what to name the fish.

CHAPTER TWENTY-THREE

ANDREW CAME to McClellan again Saturday after debate. This time, we decided to go out to eat so we could spend our time talking instead of holding hands. Well, maybe in addition to holding hands.

He picked me up at the door, exchanged a few words with my parents, and then we were free.

I loved settling into his car, the soft leather seats, its clean smell, even the small cross hanging from the rearview mirror. But I liked the guy sitting in the driver's seat even more.

He gripped my hand, then backed out of my driveway. We drove to the stoplight, and on red, he leaned over the console. "Hey."

I rubbed my nose against his. "Hey."

The light turned green, and we continued down

the street. There weren't a lot of good places to eat in town, so I pointed him toward the diner where Reese and I practiced after school. He parked right next to a familiar car. Kellum was there. And by the looks of it, a few other kids from school.

I took a deep breath. Did I really want to do this?

"Ready?" Andrew asked.

No. "Yes."

"Let me get your door."

I tried to stifle my nerves as he walked around the car, but I couldn't quite manage it.

He opened the door and leaned against the frame. At the sight of me, he frowned. "You okay?"

Andrew understood the deal with my parents. Maybe he'd get this too? "So these cars—there are some kids from my school here."

His brows furrowed. "Yeah?"

"Well, I told you I'm not really popular."

He rolled his eyes. "Skye, you're great."

I shook my head. "No, really. They might not be nice. And there have been a lot of rumors."

"We know what's true, right?" He brushed my cheek with his thumb, and I leaned into his hand. How did he always know just what to say?

"You sure?"

He nodded. "Come on. Let's go."

I took his hand and walked with him into the diner. Just like I'd guessed, about half of the seats were packed with people in my grade or above. My heart twisted to see them all laughing and joking with each other in the booths. Had no one thought to invite me?

I realized Reese and Taylor weren't there either. Knowing I wasn't the only one missing out on stuff like this didn't make it any easier. What did help, though, was the guy hanging onto my hand like he could keep me standing upright, just by being there.

He squeezed my palm. "Where do you want to sit?"

I glanced around and suggested a booth as far away from Kellum and Shelby as I could get.

The same waitress who usually waited on Reese and me approached us. "Hey, girl. He gonna make you order a coffee too?"

Andrew looked confused, and I laughed. "No, I don't think so."

"Okay, what do ya'll want to drink?"

After she took our orders, Andrew leaned back against the wall so he was sitting sideways in the booth. He played with the zipper of his jacket. "So, how was debate?"

I shrugged. "Reese and I got second in policy. I got third in informative."

His eyes lit up. "That's awesome, babe."

My heart fluttered. Babe? No one had ever called me that before.

"Thanks," I said. "It's good, but we only have two weeks to step up our game for regionals, and I don't think Reese could handle it if we don't make it to state."

I didn't add that I also wouldn't be able to handle it if we didn't make it to state. I needed debate to go to college, and I'd do whatever it took to get there.

"How'd you do?" I asked.

A sheepish grin crossed his face. "I got first in my speech."

"Oh my gosh, that's awesome!"

"Skye!" Shelby called.

I cringed.

Andrew looked over my shoulder. "Looks like they're heading this way."

"Great," I muttered.

Shelby and Kylie came to stand right in front of our table, and they grinned between Andrew and me like scheming idiots.

"Hi, there." Shelby eyed me. "So, he is real."

I rolled my eyes.

"Are you going to introduce us?" Kylie asked me then faced Shelby. "I bet Kellum would love to meet him, right?"

I looked over her shoulder and saw Kellum coming our way, fiddling with his wallet. Our eyes met, and a hurt expression crossed his visage so quickly I would have missed it if I'd blinked. How had Kylie and I ever been friends if she was the kind of person who would rub this in Kellum's face?

Kellum came to a stop behind Shelby and Kylie. "Hey." He lifted his chin in a nod.

Shelby stepped to the side so Kellum and Andrew would have a full view of each other.

Seeing the two in such close proximity was like having my worlds collide. Their similarities and differences stood out stronger than ever before—Kellum's clear charisma and Andrew's obvious gentle demeanor. Andrew with his blond hair and pink cheeks and Kellum's hard angles and shining dark eyes. Like the sun and the moon rubbing shoulders.

Shelby smiled smugly between the two of them. "This must be Skye's new boyfriend."

He already knew, though, if that flash of pain was any indication. He placed one of his easy grins on his lips and stuck out his hand. "Kellum."

Andrew nodded and shook his hand. "Andrew."

The two stared at each other for a moment, sharing a silent conversation I couldn't begin to comprehend.

Kellum shoved his hands in his pockets. "You take care of her. She's a good one."

All the breath in my lungs rushed to my head. What?

Andrew lifted his chin. "Will do, man."

Kellum nodded back—Why did guys nod so much?—and then he turned and left the diner.

Shelby and Kylie looked just as flabbergasted as I felt. After sharing a look between each other, they left behind Kellum.

Andrew took a deep drink and looked at me. "What was that about?"

I cringed. "Kellum asked me to prom, and I said no."

He appeared to be thinking for a moment, swirling the straw around his drink. "So." A slow smile spread across his face. "I got the girl?"

Laughter bubbled up in my chest. "You definitely did."

We ate together, talking and joking the entire time, swaying between heavy topics and lighter ones. I finally understood what people meant when they said they were in love with their best friend. Andrew and I could talk about anything or nothing at all, and it felt just as good either way.

On the way back to my house, we held hands across the console. He stopped at the red light and kissed me, hard, and it didn't matter that the light was about to turn green or that someone's headlights were pouring into the car.

A honk sounded behind us, and we broke apart, slowly. Andrew kept his hand on my cheek, though, and gave me another quick kiss before continuing down the road.

My driveway was already way too close. "I don't want you to go."

He chewed the inside of his cheek. "Me neither."

"Then don't." I sounded whiney, but I couldn't help it. Andrew was the best part of my week.

"I have to, babe," he said, sending my head spinning. I loved the way the words fell off his perfect lips.

"I know."

The car slowed, and we came to a stop in front of my house. I was missing him before he even left, and I needed to know when I could see him again.

"Will you be able to come next weekend?" I asked.

He frowned. "I don't know. I was going to tell you earlier, but I didn't want to ruin anything."

My stomach dropped. He was breaking up with me. I knew it—nothing this good could last. "What's going on?"

A heavy sigh blew threw his lips, the ones that looked so much better in a smile, felt so much better on mine. "My mom lost her job, and my dad...he doesn't really make enough to support us on his income. If she doesn't find something else soon, we may even have to sell the house. I'm getting a job to help—it won't be much, but I..." He ran his hand through his hair. "I won't be able to keep seeing you every weekend."

I pressed a hand over my heart. He wasn't breaking up with me, but this might have been just as bad. Not seeing Andrew, possibly over the whole summer?

My voice came out scratchy. "You'll still talk to me on the phone, right?"

He reached across the car and pulled me into him, seatbelt and all. "Every night," he said, his voice husky.

Tears pricked my eyes. "Promise?"

"Promise."

CHAPTER TWENTY-FOUR

MOM MADE a lasagna and green beans for supper Sunday, and the three of us sat around the table for the first time in months. Surprisingly, it wasn't so bad. Dad talked about a job he had lined up for the next day, I told them about prom coming up and debate, and Mom complained about one of her coworkers.

As I stood up to clear the dishes, my phone rang from my coat hanging by the door. I went to retrieve it and looked at the screen. The number wasn't saved in my contacts, but I answered anyway. "Hello?"

"Skye?"

I about dropped the phone. "Liz?"

"Yeah, it's me." There was a smile in her voice, maybe even a twinge of guilt.

"You changed your number?" Duh. I cringed at the dumb statement. Of course she had.

"Yeah," she said. "I've missed you."

My lip trembled, and tears threatened to drown my eyes. God, I'd missed her. "You too."

"Everything okay, sis?"

I glanced to where Mom and Dad sat frozen at the table. "I just... I miss you—we miss you." None of us had heard from Liz in months.

She sighed. "I don't need a guilt trip, Skye."

"No, that's not what I—"

"Don't worry about it," she sounded distracted. "I just wanted to tell you that Dorian and I eloped."

"What?"

"Like we got married last weekend."

"I know what eloping means!" I cried.

Mom stood up from the table. "Hand me the phone."

I held my finger up to Mom.

"I thought you'd be happy for me," Liz said.

"No I am, it's just—"

"Give me the phone," Mom said through gritted teeth.

"Mom, hold on, I—"

"I don't want to talk to them," Liz said. "Look, let's—"

Mom wrestled the phone from me and held it to her ear. "Liz? What did you do?"

"That's my phone!" I yelled.

"Liz!" Mom belted into the phone. "You got married without—Don't you hang up. Liz!" Mom closed her eyes, my phone still pressed against her ear. Her mouth tightened in a hard line. "That. Bitch!"

"Mom!"

Her eyes snapped open and burned into mine. "And you too."

She gripped both ends of the phone in her hands and twisted it until it snapped in half, sending shards of plastic all over the floor.

"Mom! I can't believe you just did that!" I stared from her to Dad, trying to make sense of what just happened. I'd expected something like that from Dad, but her too? "That was my phone!"

"Bill, why don't you tell our daughter who pays for that thing," she hissed.

"Dad, I—"

Dad banged his hand on the table so hard the plates rattled. "I'm so tired of this shit. Go to your room, Skye."

"What did I do?" All I could see through the red was the two halves of my phone in Mom's death grip.

"NOW!" Mom bellowed. "NOW! FUCKING NOW! GO TO YOUR ROOM!"

With a final look between the two, I ran out of the kitchen. A lump made of glass and unshed tears stabbed at my throat. That had been my last connection to the only person in my life who really liked me, wanted to know me, believed in me.

And they'd taken it away.

I hated them.

And Liz.

And every bit of this stupid freaking situation I never chose for myself.

CHAPTER TWENTY-FIVE

I HAD an appointment with Dr. Pike Monday, and I was not looking forward to two hours in the car with Mom.

She picked me up from school around noon, and we drove in charged silence for the first hour of the trip. She and Dad had fought all evening about Liz eloping and said all sorts of horrible things about how the other parented, all the while ruining the life of the one daughter who still lived with them.

Around half an hour outside of Austin, I broke the silence. "How was your day?"

The question seemed innocuous enough, but Mom glared at me.

"What?" I asked.

She shook her head. "I don't even know where

my daughter lives anymore. Didn't know she was getting married, don't even know her phone number."

I wanted to point out that Mom had destroyed the one thing that could have given her at least one piece of that information, but I didn't want to make her angry. Well, angrier. I had to find out how to get my phone replaced—how to connect myself to Andrew and maybe even Liz.

"I miss Liz," I admitted.

Mom scoffed. "Like she cares."

Outrage dominated my mind. I'd thought the same thing about Liz a million times, but she was my sister. No one else could talk crap about her except me.

"That's not true," I said.

"Really? When's the last time you heard from her before that? She come see you before your surgery? Did she go to any of your volleyball games? No. The only time we hear from her is when she wants something."

And now, I was upset for more than one reason, because my mom was trash talking the sister I needed, the sister she and Dad drove away. And that sister had been in touch with them at some point, and I'd never known about it, never had a chance to even say hi. "What has she asked you for?"

"How is that any of your business?"

Mom kept her eyes forward, and I did the same.

Asking for anything now wouldn't end well. I pretended to read for the rest of the trip, but the entire time, I thought about Liz and the life she was able to lead just because she got away and never looked back.

The appointment with Dr. Pike went just like before. He gave me a new set of exercises to add to my routine, told me not to worry about my weight gain, asked Mom how Dad and Branch were doing, then sent us home. The only difference was he said I could take my brace off when I was around the house and stop wearing it in public in three weeks.

In the car, I decided there was no time like the present.

"Mom?" I started.

She stopped at the sign leading out of the hospital's parking garage. "Yes?"

"While we're in town, could we pick up a new phone for me?"

She looked left and right then pulled onto the street. "Who's paying for it?"

"Um. You and Dad? It wasn't my fault it broke."

"It kind of was."

"Because I answered my phone?"

"No," she snapped. "Because you refuse to follow instructions. If you want a phone, you need to pay for it."

My mouth fell open. I hardly had time to eat, much less work a regular part-time job and sleep.

She glanced over at me. "Close your mouth. You look stupid."

"Are you kidding me? I go to school eight hours a day, keep a 4.0 grade point average, and then stay after for two hours to work on things that will help me pay for college since you and Dad can't. How am I supposed to find time for a job too?"

"If you want a phone, you'll figure it out."

Anger boiled up my chest and spilled out my mouth. "This is crap! It's not my fault Liz called me and not you!"

"Stop it right now," Mom hissed.

"Why? Truth hurts? You lost your temper and broke something just like Dad always does. You're just as bad as he is!"

She swerved as she turned to yell at me, "STOP IT RIGHT NOW!"

A car honked, but Mom kept it up.

"You're an ungrateful little brat who thinks she

should just lay on the couch and have the world handed to her on a silver platter. What? You're worried about missing your little boyfriend? It's not like it's going to last longer than a month anyway. And if you weren't constantly causing problems and bringing up drama, your father and I wouldn't fight as much as we do. You think this whole surgery thing has been easy on us? It's put us thousands of dollars into debt, just so you could play your little games."

"'Little games?'" I screamed. "Your and Dad's poor finances are the whole reason I play those 'little games,' so I can get away from you!"

"You have to be good for it to matter, and I hate to break it to you, but fat girls don't play college sports."

I gasped and said the most hurtful thing I could muster. "Liz did the right thing getting away from you."

"No one's hoping you'll stick around either."

I couldn't handle being around her, couldn't handle sitting next to her. I pulled my hood over my head, moved as near the door as I could get, and stared out the window. I wouldn't let her ruin my life like she and Dad had ruined theirs.

Andrew was right—I couldn't control my situation, but I could control my future.

CHAPTER TWENTY-SIX

ALL DAY I worried about Andrew and what he thought of my inability to communicate. Yeah, it was my first time with a boyfriend, but I knew other people my age freaked out if they couldn't get in touch with someone they were dating.

After school, I met Reese at the diner. He already had a stack of research in front of him and a cup of coffee for me.

"Hey." I slid into the booth. "I'm going to have to miss practice tomorrow."

He raised his eyebrows like I'd just confessed to a horrible crime. "Regionals are in two weeks. What on earth could possibly be more important than practice?"

Now I felt embarrassed. "It's kind of a long story."

"Well, go on, it's not like we have anything more important to be doing." He glanced down at his watch and pushed a button.

"Wait, are you timing me?"

He waved his hand in a carry-on gesture.

I rolled my eyes. "Look Reese, my parents broke my phone. I'm dating this guy from Woodman, and I haven't been able to talk to him in like three days—"

He glared at the ceiling.

"I wouldn't expect you to understand, but he's my first real boyfriend, and I don't want to ruin it. So, I'll have to miss tomorrow. Give me extra research or something at school—I'll make it up."

His lips twisted to the side, then he placed both of his hands on the table and looked me squarely in the eyes. "Skye, I'm going to compliment you. Don't let it go to your head, okay?"

I scrunched my eyebrows but nodded.

"Okay." He blew out a breath. "You're a great debater. You might even be better than Taylor. If you keep at it, I could see us winning state next year, and that opens up all sorts of opportunities that would be...otherwise impossible for you to come by."

My heart fell. Reese saw it, just like everyone

else saw it. My second-hand clothes, run-down home on the outskirts of a nowhere town, how desperately I wanted to be anywhere but here.

"Promise me you'll put that first and not let whatever romantic interest you have right now ruin that. And by all means, please, practice safe sex. Although they only have an eighty percent success rate, you can buy condoms at almost any gas station bathroom, Walmart, Walgreens, I mean, the list goes on. No reason not to use them, and if this loser refuses—"

"Reese!" I cried, my cheeks getting redder by the second. "I am *so* not there yet. But, duly noted."

Seemingly satisfied, he nodded then glanced at his watch. "Seven minutes and thirty-two seconds. Not bad, Hoffner."

"Don't stop your time yet."

He sighed. "What now?"

"Well, can I use your phone to text him and tell him what's going on?"

Reese held up the latest version of the iPhone, its surface so perfectly clean I couldn't even detect a fingerprint. "Does this phone look like I let anyone else use it?"

"Come on, Reese."

He shook his head. "No, but I'll send him a

message on Facebook. I wouldn't want just anyone having my number."

I rolled my eyes. "Fine. Look up Andrew Brindon."

Reese whipped a stylus out of his pocket and tapped at the screen. "Okay, what would you like me to send him?"

"Um. You can just say, 'Hi, I'm sending you this because I'm too stuck up to get someone else's germs on my phone'"—Reese glared at me—"'Skye's parents broke her cell, but she's getting a new phone as soon as possible and will send you a message when she does.'"

He finally finished tapping his stylus across the screen and cleared his throat. "'Hi Andrew, you might not know me, but I am Skye Hoffner's debate partner. She sends you the following message: Dear Andrew, My parents have broken my phone beyond repair. I am working to get a new phone as soon as possible and will contact you at that time. Dictated but not read, Skye Hoffner.'"

"Sure." I sighed. "Will you let me know if he replies?"

I wouldn't be able to talk to Andrew soon enough. I needed to tell someone who would understand about all the crap that had gone down since Liz called.

"Yes," Reese said. "But it's been ten minutes and twenty-four seconds. Can we get started now?"

For the next two hours, Reese drilled me endlessly with different arguments, some logical, some insane. He said I needed to be prepared for every situation with logical sources to combat every illogical argument. According to Reese, the judges often got swept up in the emotional presentation of it all unless the case was so strong and apparent they'd feel dumb not to side with reason.

After our practice, my head burned, my eyelids felt heavy, and I was ready to have a bite to eat and fall straight asleep.

Unfortunately, my parents had another idea.

CHAPTER TWENTY-SEVEN

THE SECOND I walked through the door, they pounced on me.

Mom held up an envelope. "Got your ACT scores. Thirty."

My brows lifted. Thirty? That was three points higher than the last time!

Both she and Dad scowled at me, and Dad took the letter from her. "Says here you took it at 'Upton Collegiate Testing Center in Austin, Texas.'"

Oh God. I hadn't thought about this. About the fact I'd be getting mail and my parents didn't believe in leaving any letter unopened for me to read.

I fought to keep my expression even. "You opened my mail?"

Dad growled. "It's addressed to my house, I have

the right to open it. Now tell us what the hell you were doing in Austin."

My stomach boiled with nerves. "Taking the ACT."

"And they didn't have it here?"

I blinked slowly. Once. Twice. It was a small town—I was lucky news about Kellum and me hadn't already reached them. "I wanted to take it in Austin to see Upton, and someone offered to drive me, so I didn't have to spend any gas money."

A vein in Dad's neck bobbed right below the surface of his skin. "Who was it?"

I tried to say Kellum, but my voice came out as a rasp, so I cleared my throat. "Kellum Watts."

Mom and Dad looked at each other.

Mom said, "You went on a date." It wasn't a question.

"Kind of," I admitted.

This was ridiculous. I'd gotten a thirty, *a thirty*, on my ACT, and they were grilling me about who I'd taken it with. Kids who scored thirty on the ACT got into any college they wanted, they got scholarships, opportunities, a life outside of McClellan. But Dad's face was growing redder by the second.

"You were sneaking around with boys, just like

your sister did, and look how she ended up. A broke, married, loser."

"Sounds like someone else I know." I covered my mouth immediately. What had I just said?

Dad gripped the paper, ripped, and kicked the recliner. "Grounded."

"What?"

"You heard me!" he roared. "Grounded! You go to school on the bus, you come home on the bus, you stay in your room, and you go to work like me."

"What about debate practice?" I argued. "Prom?"

"I don't know how you're supposed to get there without a car. But if you think you're such an adult, you figure it out." He downed his glass. "Now get outside and bring me your keys."

"Dad, I—"

He threw his glass against the wall, and it shattered into a million sparkling pieces. "Get outside and bring me your keys," he hissed, his voice low. The calm before the storm that would obliterate everything in its path. Including me.

I spun to go outside and felt paper hitting my back. My scores.

Outside, I heard Dad roar through the door.

I walked down the sidewalk, shaking the entire way.

I should have left, should have gotten in my pickup, turned the ignition, and driven as far as I could. But for whatever stupid reason, I pulled my keys, walked inside, handed them to Dad with my chin up, and stormed to my room.

And then I promptly fell apart.

CHAPTER TWENTY-EIGHT

FOR THE NEXT TWO WEEKS, I did as my parents said. I rode the bus to school in the mornings, Reese drove me home after debate practice, and I worked with Dad on every odd job he had that wasn't during school or debate.

Reese had messaged Anika, and she said she and Brandon would be meeting me at the school before prom Saturday. But Andrew still hadn't messaged Reese back, and I hadn't had a chance to get a new phone and message him myself.

If I'd thought what happened during volleyball season was bad, I was kidding myself. This. This was as bad as it could get.

I had no one to talk to. Not a single soul who I could tell, much less anyone who would understand.

Before this mess, I would have talked to Kylie or Sheldon. Kylie would have invited me over, and we'd have spent the night pigging out on one of her mom's homemade desserts and talking about boys or volleyball or music. And Sheldon would have known exactly what to say to make me feel better, but we were worse than strangers now. Not friends, not quite enemies.

I just had to hope that the one person who had cared, Andrew, would still be there when I finally saw him again.

When I was working on debate, impossible doubts and fears attacked my mind. With regionals coming up, I couldn't afford to let everything else sidetrack me like Reese had warned.

Mrs. Grady agreed to read over my speech after school Monday to help me fine-tune the grammar and word choice. The rest of the week, I spent my time after school in Mrs. Grady's classroom with Mr. Yen and the rest of the debate team, practicing debate procedure and working over my speech. Reese and I spent extra time during the meetings continuing our practice together.

At home, I ate, showered, finished my homework, then I stood in front of my mirror to practice the speeches. Bed time turned out to be around 10:30

every night. I would fall back into my bed so mentally exhausted I barely had the time or energy to think about Andrew.

Mr. Yen and I were going over my speech the day before regionals when he stopped me.

"Don't change your speech anymore," he said. "Just go home, go over it in your mind, and get a good night's rest before tomorrow. Regionals and prom in one day is going to be tough."

━━━

Groaning softly, I dropped my feet over the edge of the bed and sat up, rubbing the poor night's sleep out of my eyes. I'd tossed and turned, unable to sleep soundly with the weight of regionals pressing on my chest.

Dad's snoring seeped in under my door, and I sighed. There was a pretty good chance he and Mom wouldn't even be awake by the time I left.

As they slept, I went into the bathroom, getting ready for the day. I tucked my frizzy curls into a bun, coated my lashes in mascara, and used a generous amount of concealer to hide the stress and exhaustion practically leaking out my pores.

I already had my bag packed and my prom dress

over my arm when Dad stumbled sleepily toward the coffee pot.

"You're up early," he said, scratching the stubble on his chin.

I nodded. "I have debate today and then prom tonight."

"You got a ride squared?"

"Yeah. Reese said he'd pick me up."

"Heading out?"

I adjusted my bag so it rested more comfortably over my shoulder. "Yeah."

Over the sound of water dripping into the coffee pot, he said, "Break a leg."

"Thanks, Dad." I nodded and walked out the door, realizing that was the first civil conversation we'd had since he'd thrown my ACT test scores at my back.

I wished I had a few more minutes to wait on a cup of coffee and chat. This early, before the world got started, it was almost like we could be a normal dad and daughter. Like we could both pretend we had the kind of relationship where he cheered me on and I didn't have to walk on eggshells around him.

As it was, Reese and I barely made it to the school on time, and the bus left shortly after we got in.

We had to sit near the back of the bus, but I didn't mind because everyone stayed quiet, like the blue light right before sunrise and the warm air pouring through the vents had sedative properties.

I leaned my head back against the seat and thought over the research I'd reviewed the night before. I didn't want to give anything less than my best. This could be my last meet of the season. Nerves overtook my stomach. This time next year, I'd be a senior. State this year could be my one chance to impress college coaches.

The bus came to a stop in Rowley High School's parking lot, and we piled out. I stretched my legs, trying to get some blood flow to my feet. My knee ached from being cramped up for so long. All the blood settled on my heart, pounding anxiously.

"Ready?" Mr. Yen asked, thumbing through a stack of papers.

I nodded, not trusting my voice. Last time I'd been this nervous, I had an anesthesia mask over my face.

Reese looked pale, too, belying his steady voice. "Of course."

We followed Mr. Yen through the doors and into the early morning chaos. He said he would check us in and told us to go find a table.

The halls filled with so many students I had to guard my knee to keep people from bumping into me. None of our meets had been this crowded. Knowing Andrew was performing at another meet somehow helped, like our shared experiences bonded us even when we couldn't talk. I hoped he'd make it to state so I could explain, if it came down to that.

Our small group wound our way through the crush of students and finally found an empty end of a bench table in the cafeteria. We spread our bags and papers out so no one would encroach on our space.

Taylor flipped her binder open. "Okay, we should go over our research and speeches."

"Agreed." Reese looked at me. "Mr. Yen should have our position soon, so we need to use our time as best as we can."

I nodded, settling in beside him. Something had changed since we started working together. I felt a little less jealous of all he had, and being partners made me feel more driven, somehow, closer to success.

"Can I read through some of your articles?" I asked.

"Yeah." He pulled a stack of stapled papers from

a pocket in his binder. "I haven't had a chance to look at these yet."

I took them from him and started skimming the small print. These articles always seemed so dense, but I focused on each word until I got the general picture and made notes in the margins.

Mr. Yen approached us, brandishing a stack of colored papers. "I got your assignments. Reese and Skye, you're one of the first teams on the schedule, so you need to head to the library..."

The rest of what he said about the others' events was lost on me as Reese and I gathered our materials and left the table. Reese had this rolling briefcase akin to something you'd see with a businessman in an airport, and it clacked over each tile as we walked through the crowd.

After we arrived and got our assignment, we meticulously organized our arguments, made quick notes, and ran through an expedited practice between the two of us.

Reese gave me some pointers on my delivery, and I told him when he needed to speak in less technical terms so the judges could clearly understand our stance.

"8:27," he said. "You ready?"

I nodded, feeling my stomach dangle from my esophagus heavier than a heap of bricks.

We gathered our materials and walked to the conference room we were scheduled to debate in.

Our opponents, a couple of guys in black suits with more hair gel than mobsters, stood outside the door. When we approached, they squared their shoulders. One of them, the tall, skinny one, stuck his hand out, and Reese shook it. His partner and I followed suit, greeting each other and shaking hands.

A man peeked his head out the conference room door. "Ready?"

I took a deep breath. "As we'll ever be."

We stepped in and took our side of the room. I spread my binder out in front of me and used the sound of Reese's breath to steady my pulse. No one sat in the few chairs provided for an audience, but I still felt nervous. This—debate—it was my chance at going to college. I needed to do well.

The man asked if we were ready again, and when we said we were, he reminded us of the procedure and set a timer. The affirmative side always went first, so Reese gave our opening statement, preforming even better than we had practiced. He transformed when he spoke from a snobby teenager into an expert with a firm grasp on GMOs and labeling issues.

At the conclusion of his argument, the opposition had some time to discuss, then the taller guy got up and asked Reese a series of tricky, in-depth questions. Reese held his own for the questioning, then came to sit by me. I nudged his arm with my elbow.

"Good job," I whispered.

His lips twitched at the corners, but he kept his gaze forward. "Thanks."

We had researched, but so had they. The taller opponent stepped to the podium and gave one of the most impassioned speeches I was sure the world had ever heard about GMO labeling.

If there had been more people in the room, I bet they would have clapped as the guy finished, gathered his notes, and sat back down. Heck, I bet they would have given him a standing ovation.

Reese and I bent our heads over our binders, trying to come up with questions for his position, which had been about as airtight as a vacuum. We came up with a few inquiries that he easily batted off.

The time came for my turn, and I wanted to do anything but stand at the podium and pretend I knew what I was talking about. I couldn't compete with that.

"You've got this," Reese breathed.

I nodded, swallowing back every bit of acid nerves I felt. Taking my time, I picked up my binder, went to the podium, and tried to let everything fade away except for me, my notes, and the judge sitting in front of me.

He wore glasses with thick brown frames, and his eyes were a warm brown, like melting chocolate chips. Not as bright as Kellum's, but almost.

I took a deep breath, nodded to start my time, and presented the best I knew how. At the end of my turn, I stood at the podium, waiting for the assault of questions.

I dodged each one, and only stumbled over my answer once. I went back to the table with Reese to prepare for the next step.

He grinned at me over our notes. "Nice work, Hoffner."

After the debate, I felt energized. We wouldn't know the results until the judge submitted them, but I felt like Reese and I had held our own against the toughest debaters we'd met all season.

Reese and I started toward the cafeteria. His rolling bag clacked behind us as we worked our way back to our team. I still had to present my informative speech, he had to do an extemporaneous speech, and time was running short in the round.

Once we were out of earshot of our opponents, Reese grinned at me. "That was awesome. I haven't been up against anyone that good in a long time."

"I bet they place at state," I said.

Reese bumped my arm, reminding me, "They can't go to state if we won."

I frowned, coming back to reality. "And we can't if they won."

We got back to the table and moved on to our next performances. If there was one thing I'd learned by doing debate, it was that staying in the zone helped build momentum. I stood facing a wall and practiced my speech once more, and Reese rushed off to his event.

According to the schedule, I had to go to Room 201C. Finding it proved difficult, but only because I'd assumed I'd be presenting in a classroom. Wrong. They'd put me in what equated to a storage closet.

A small, mousy woman sat at a desk that barely fit inside, flipping through a book, and I peeked my head in. "Informative?"

She read to the end of her page, nodding as she shut the book. "Right. Are you Hoffner or Bronton?"

"Hoffner."

"Good." She made a mark on a piece of paper, then pulled out a legal pad. "I'm ready when you are."

"Alrighty." I stepped in and closed the door behind me, despite my rising claustrophobia. I bet if I extended my arms I could touch both walls.

"It's a tight space," she said, apparently catching my unease, "but just do your best."

I nodded, took a deep breath, and stared down at the floor. In debate events, the time started after you looked at the floor, then to the judge, and started talking.

I followed the ritual and began with the opening of my speech. "I was playing basketball, defending the best JV point guard this side of Dallas, when I heard a crack, followed by the worst pain I've ever felt in my life. I didn't know it then, but I'd experienced..."

She watched as I moved about the small space, sharing the details of ACL injuries, cures, and statistics. Her eyes turned watery at the close when I spoke about recovery times after surgery and crushed dreams.

Mrs. Grady had said tying in the emotional aspect of physical injuries would draw the judges in, and so far, she had been right. I finished speaking, nodded, and thanked her for the opportunity to share my topic with her.

"Nice work," she said, smiling, "and you have my wishes for a speedy recovery."

"Thank you," I said. "It means more than you know."

Shaking from nerves and the adrenaline of performing, I stopped at a water fountain to soothe my throat. I'd given all I had because every performance could be my last at this point, and I wasn't leaving anything on the table.

Back at the cafeteria, nearly my entire team sat together, except for Reese and Mr. Yen. The round had to be nearly over, so I expected Reese would be back from performing soon.

"Where's Mr. Yen?" I asked Taylor.

She crunched on a carrot stick. "Getting scores, I think."

I nodded and opened my binder in front of me. I wouldn't know until he came back with the results whether I actually needed to keep reviewing my research, but I went over the pages Reese had given me that morning, just in case.

Reese came back before Mr. Yen and plopped into his chair. "One round down, two to go."

"For extemp," I said. "We'll see if we moved on or not."

His face took on a grim expression. "They were really good."

Taylor patted his arm. "You guys are good, though."

He dropped his head to the side and gave her a sarcastic, "Thanks."

We sat in a quiet, fidgety group until Mr. Yen came back. We must have looked like sunflowers following the sun as he walked into the cafeteria and toward our table.

"Good news and bad news," he said, pulling out a chair and setting a folder in front of him. "Policy, Reese and Skye, you lost. By one point."

My heart plummeted. We'd poured hours into practice, and our team had been broken up, just like that.

"Those guys are good," Mr. Yen said. "Their coach said they're undefeated. I think you just played the championship round."

Reese tugged off his suit jacket and threw it over the back of his chair. "One point. One measly point?"

I got what he was saying. It almost hurt more to know we were so close. Just one different move could have tipped the balance.

"You need some good news," Mr. Yen said. "Reese, you took first in the round in extemp. Skye, second. Nice work..."

He told the rest of our teammates their scores, but none of them had scored as high as Reese and me. He and I might be going to state together, just not as a team.

By the third round, both Reese and I were leading in the score. We were the only two on the team to secure a spot in finals, and Mr. Yen took a meeting with us privately before our last performances.

The three of us stood in what seemed like the only empty corner of the school—an open space under a stairwell. Reese had his rolling bag of resources with him, and my hands were painfully empty. I folded them over my chest just for something to do.

"You two are the best debaters our school's seen in a long time," Mr. Yen began, and my heart buoyed from its funk. "And you're only juniors. Any college would be lucky to have you two, and you'll be a formidable force at state if you make it. But I want you to forget all that. I want you two to go into this round and do the best you can. Forget the rest."

He paused, looking at us until he had caught both our gazes. "You understand?"

"Yes, sir," Reese said.

"Yes," I breathed.

Adrenaline coursed through me, making even my ankles feel shaky, but Mr. Yen's words brought some calm back to my senses. He was right. I knew I could speak well, I knew my speech. I was ready.

Mr. Yen put his hands on both of our shoulders. "Go get 'em."

I turned to Reese. "Good luck."

He stuck his hand out, and I took it. "You've got this, Hoffner."

"I hope so, Shiloh."

We gave each other a final nod before going to our respective destinations.

Instead of letting my thoughts wander, I counted each tile I stepped on. At number 43, I stood in front of the room—an actual classroom this time instead of a closet.

I walked through the open door and saw students and parents sitting in the desks, plus three judges up front.

Taking a deep breath, I turned back toward the door and closed it, using the moment to gather myself, then I turned back toward the judges. "Skye Hoffner, McClellan High."

The judge closest to me, a woman with the smoothest hair I'd ever seen, said, "I've got you down."

The other two made similar remarks.

Then she said, "We're ready when you are."

My hands grew sweaty at the sight of at least ten sets of eyes staring straight at me. I lowered my head toward the floor, white tiles with false gray pebbles painted on, and then looked back at the audience and started speaking.

The judges' eyes followed me with each step, and I made sure to make eye contact with each of them like Mr. Yen told me to. I spoke loudly enough for everyone in the room to hear me and enunciated each of my words.

At the close of my speech, a polite smattering of applause reached my ears. I thanked the judges, and I walked out. Another girl about my age waited outside.

"It went well?" she asked, chewing on her lips, resulting in a red lipstick stain on her front two teeth.

"Yeah." I nodded. "Good luck."

She nodded and moved toward the door.

"Hey," I said, causing her to stop mid-step. "You have a little lipstick on your tooth."

Her eyes instantly flooded, and her hand flew to her teeth, rubbing. "Oh my gosh, thank you. That would have been so bad."

She flashed her now lipstickless smile at me. "Did I get it?"

I nodded again. "Break a leg."

"You too," she said, then her eyes found my brace. "Well, looks like you already have."

She turned toward the room, and her shoulders rose and fell under her blazer.

I walked as slowly as I could back to the cafeteria, allowing my mind to imagine the whole way. Imagine that my leg was better. Imagine that I'd win. Imagine that a scholarship could take me far, far away from here.

CHAPTER TWENTY-NINE

REESE DROPPED into the seat in front of me on the bus and rested his arm on its back. "Hey."

I smiled at him. "Hey yourself."

A soft, relieved smile touched his eyes more than his lips. "You did really good today."

"I'm sorry we didn't make it in policy debate."

He shrugged. "Mr. Yen was right. We played the championship round and got bested by one point. Can't really ask for better than that."

I nodded. "Yeah."

"Good job on your speech."

My heart lifted. "Thanks."

"Second place isn't bad. And you'll do great at state."

I smiled wide. "Don't you mean, 'we'll do great at state'?"

The circles under his eyes were darker today. Regionals must have put more pressure on him than he let on earlier. Still, his shoulders looked like some of the weight had been removed. "Yeah, that's what I meant." He leaned closer and whispered. "I'm actually kind of glad it's just us. I feel like...I don't know. Like we're the two people who want it the most."

If he only knew how much I wanted it.

We stayed quiet for a moment, examining each other.

"Still no word from Andrew?" I asked.

With a frown, he shook his head. "No, I even resent the message so he'd get another notification, but no dice."

"Did it show up as seen?"

"Nope. But that doesn't really mean much."

I looked down at my hands resting in my lap with no fingernail polish and callouses from working with Dad and lifting weights. Was it something about me?

Reese dragged me out of my thoughts. "We're going to have fun at prom, right?"

I laughed. "Kylie and Brittany worked way too hard for us not to."

For the first time in my life, I watched Reese roll his eyes. It seemed totally unnatural, out of character. "How were you ever friends with her?" He shook his head. "You've chosen much better company this semester."

It wasn't really my choice, but, "Thanks."

A sense of finality hung between us, and Reese turned and went back to the front of the bus. Probably to talk strategy with Mr. Yen for state. We had a couple weeks to prepare, but it didn't feel like nearly enough time.

Taylor dropped into the seat across from me. "Please help. I can't believe we only have an hour and a half to get ready for prom."

I'd planned on just changing into my dress at school and maybe touching up my mascara, but Taylor had a giant bag of makeup in front of her. What was it with every girl my age having an endless supply of eyeshadow, blush, and bronzer?

"Sure thing," I said. "What were you thinking?"

Right up until we pulled into the school's parking lot, we stayed busy spraying and pinning her hair, brushing on all colors of makeup, and gluing on fake nails. Taylor even sprayed me with some of her glitter. It looked a little ridiculous with my debate clothes, but it would go well with my gown.

All us girls went into the locker room and changed into our dresses, and it struck me how different things were this year from the year before. Last prom, I had been on top of the world; I'd had great friends I could trust with my life, and my prom date was James, a 6'4" hunk who'd come to pick me up in his nice, freshly washed and waxed pickup. He'd held my hand on the way home to drop me off and even gave me a quick peck goodnight.

None of that would be happening this year. Instead of riding into prom with a hot guy, I'd pulled up in a yellow school bus, and not even in a cool, ironic way. Not to mention my "date" was a pair of out-of-town friends who basically wanted to come out of pity.

We walked out of the locker room, and I went to wait by the front doors to greet Anika and Brandon. Reese was standing there, too, probably waiting on someone.

"You look great," he told me sincerely, making me feel bad for being so negative about him in the past.

He looked...really good. He wore a suit, not a tux, that must have cost as much as my pickup. The cool gray material had clearly been tailored to his slim frame, and his high cheekbones made him look even more like he belonged at a GQ photoshoot instead of at a high school prom.

"You look nice too," I said.

"Who're you waiting on?" he asked.

"Some of my friends are coming. You?"

The tips of his ears gained a red hue, and he mumbled something inaudible.

"What was that?"

He frowned. "Don't make me say it."

"What?" I laughed. "Are you bringing your cousin or something?"

The pained look on his face told me I'd guessed correctly.

"But don't you dare tell anyone, Hoffner," he warned.

I made a cross over my sweetheart neckline. "But you couldn't have asked anyone else? Surely Taylor or Paige would—"

"My mom is making me. She's homeschooled, so she doesn't get to go to anything like this."

"Well, that explains things." I laughed.

He scoffed. "Research suggests homeschooled students perform just as well or better academically as publicly schooled students, and, well, as to the social aspect, you of all people should know that public school doesn't necessarily—"

A girl in an intricately beaded red dress approached the door.

"Ah, that's her," he said. He held it open for her. "Mary Elizabeth."

The family resemblance between them was uncanny. She was just as thin as him, with a dainty collarbone accented by a pearl necklace. She held her chin high, like she'd been in ballet for years.

"Reese," she said. She cast me a sideways glance down her nose. "Who is she?"

Reese rolled his eyes for the second time that day. "Don't be such a snob."

He gave me a pained look and led her toward the gym.

I found myself laughing quietly at the pair. Reese calling someone else a snob? There was a first for everything.

Anika and Brandon came through the doors next, Anika in a beautiful orange gown and Brandon looking impishly handsome in a simple black suit.

Anika immediately hugged me, and I squeezed her back.

"How's everything?" she asked.

I looked toward the ceiling. "It hasn't been great."

"Come on," she said and looped her arm through

mine. "Let's go take pictures. And tell us everything."

I started with my sister calling and finished with Andrew's lack of response. My eyes stung with unshed tears, and I had to breathe deeply and blink fast to stop them from falling and ruining what little makeup I had on.

Anika squeezed my shoulder. "One year left, girl."

It would never be soon enough.

When we got in line to take pictures, our conversation stalled as we looked at all the dresses around us. My least favorite part of prom was always the pictures and the promenade. For two minutes each, the photographer places the couples in an awkward pose, instructs them to tilt their heads at some odd angle, then snaps a picture that won't do justice to the hours upon hours spent getting ready. Meanwhile, all of the parents stand around chatting and reliving their own high school memories. Three strikes: no dancing, parents, and too much small talk.

I glanced over at Kellum more times than I cared to admit. He and Saffron had already made it through pictures and sat together at a table with a group of seniors. They were totally absorbed in each other. Saffron even picked up a cookie and fed it to him. Ugh.

Finally, the lights dimmed, and the dance started. For the first few songs, Anika, Brandon, and I danced together. But then Anika spotted Rhett with Savannah and her friends, and we had a group of nearly eight people fast dancing together. It felt good to have a circle of friends around me, dancing to the music. But the whole time, I couldn't help but think about Andrew at his own prom.

Who was he dancing with? Was he having a good time? Had he thought of me at all?

For the slow dances, Anika and I took turns with Brandon, but she also got asked to dance by a few guys from my school. Eventually, Savannah was dancing with someone in her class, and Rhett asked me to dance.

It was a slow country song, and Rhett knew every word. At first, he sang along, and I got lost in his voice.

At a break in the song, I said, "You need to be a singer."

He laughed. "Not hardly."

"Yes. If Carrie Underwood can win American Idol, you can too."

He laughed harder. "No way."

We spun in a slow circle near Kellum and Saffron who danced nose to nose. He had his hand wound underneath her waterfall curls, and she had a soft smile as she whispered to him.

Rhett nodded toward them. "Looks like you made your decision."

I shrugged. "I mean, yeah, but it didn't exactly work out like I'd planned."

"Where's the other guy?" he asked. "Andrew?"

I closed my eyes and my lids turned red as a light passed over us. "You mean my boyfriend?"

I opened my eyes to see Rhett's confused expression. "What do you mean?"

I told Rhett about my parents taking my phone and Andrew never responding to any of Reese's messages. "And I have no idea how to get in touch with him and tell him what's going on."

My chest tightened with each word, and now I could hardly breathe. Rhett probably didn't know his arms around my waist were all that was keeping me up.

He frowned. "You know his number, right?"

I nodded.

"Well." He pulled his phone out of his pocket. "Call him."

I gasped. "Really?"

He nodded.

I wrapped my arms around him and gave him a hug. "I'll be right back."

"Go," he said. "But you better be a little sorry for leaving me in the middle of the dance floor."

I glanced toward a few of the girls along the edges of the gym staring wistfully at Rhett. "I'm pretty sure you'll be alright."

He tilted his head toward the door. "Call him."

I gave him a grateful smile, bunched up my dress, and made my escape for the girls' bathroom.

It was like the pattern of Andrew's number had burned itself into my brain, and my fingers were programmed to type it in. I flipped open Rhett's cell —the kind that was supposed to be indestructible— and swiftly entered the numbers.

A call failure tone beeped through the phone. "The number you have dialed has been disconnected. Please hang up and try again later."

I stared at the screen. Surely, I'd entered in the wrong number. It looked right, but it had to have been wrong.

I typed the number again, more slowly this time, and pressed send.

The tone beeped through the phone.

"No," I whispered. "No, no, no."

I redialed. And redialed. And redialed. But the tone never changed.

My stomach churned, and I ran into a stall, falling to my knees and bending over a toilet. Everything I'd eaten that day swirled in my stomach acid, threatening to come up.

Disconnected? Had Andrew changed his number? I swallowed. Had he changed it so I couldn't get in touch with him?

A more logical thought crossed my mind: Andrew's parents were having money troubles. Maybe they hadn't kept up with the bill. Or maybe they'd changed services. I just needed to send him another message on Facebook. Or hope I'd see him at state.

My stomach settled slightly with the thought, and I stood up and brushed off the front of my dress as best I could. I met Brandon and Anika back at the dance and joined them in a fast song like nothing had happened. I could tell them about it later. Right now, I just wanted to be normal and dance with my friends at prom, like my biggest worry was waking up at noon the next day to do homework.

And I succeeded. At the end of the dance, the lights flipped on, and Anika, Brandon, and I stood together.

"So, are we going to after prom or what?" Anika asked.

"Yep. We can ride together, right?" I asked.

Anika raised her eyebrows. "It's not here?"

"No, my class rented out the movie theater."

Bran's eyes lit up. "What are we watching? Did the guys get a say?"

Anika smacked him on the shoulder. "Let's hope not."

"It's a comedy, I think. Some of the moms picked it."

They looked at each other, and Bran nodded. Anika whacked his shoulder again, and they laughed, never saying a word. I wished I had a friend that knew me so well we didn't even have to speak to be understood.

"We can take my car," Bran offered.

"Can we go change at your house first?" Anika asked. "I need to take off these eyelashes."

"Oh, well, I—my house isn't really very...nice," I finished lamely.

She batted her hand. "We don't care what your house looks like."

Saffron had said almost exactly the same thing before she came over, and look where we were now. She was dating the guy she knew I had a crush on, and I was miserable. But I'd do anything to keep Anika and Brandon as friends—even lie.

"Let's change in the locker room. If we go to my house, we'll get there too late."

Anika and I went to the girls' locker room, and Bran went to the guys'. When Anika and I finished changing, Brandon was already waiting outside the locker room, looking comfortable in some sweats and a t-shirt.

"Ready to go?" he asked.

I shrugged.

Anika nodded. "Let's go."

We drove to the movie theater with the music too loud to talk. It was a newer song I hadn't heard since I didn't have the radio anymore, but Anika and Brandon sang to every word. Soon enough, we pulled up and got out.

Most of the seats were already full, and we found a few empty ones together toward the front. Brandon joked the entire way through the movie, which probably would have stunk without his wisecracks.

Afterwards, they asked if I wanted to cruise. And since there was about zero chance of my parents staying up this late to wait on us, I said sure.

Minutes into our first pass down Main, my stress

about Andrew spilled over, and I told them about my failed attempts to call him.

Brandon handed his phone to me. "Check out his Facebook. Maybe you'll see something there?"

He turned the car out of town, and the phone seemed to grow brighter as the streetlights around us faded away.

I didn't even bother logging into my own account —I just pulled up Andrew's page. Surprisingly—or not—Brandon and Andrew were Facebook friends. I guessed it made sense, considering Brandon had more than a thousand friends compared to the measly few hundred I had.

Finally, Andrew's page loaded. The first thing I saw was his profile picture. It was about a year and a half old and didn't do justice to the way he looked now. When the picture had been taken, his cheeks were fuller and lacked some of the harder edges age had given him. His hair was cut better now, in a way that accentuated his waves instead of making them look messy.

I scrolled down his page to see if anything new had happened. A girl, Stormy, posted on his page.

Stormy Rodriguez: Congrats on making it to STATE, babe! So proud of you!

My heart stuttered to a stop. Friends could call each other babe, right?

At the next update, I dropped the phone. "Oh my god."

Anika twisted in the seat. "What?"

"Pull over!" I yelled at Brandon.

This time I really was going to be sick.

He slowed the car, but not fast enough. My stomach churned, my heart was ripping into tattered confetti, and my mind was the worst place I could imagine being.

"Pull over!" I yelled again, and he swerved the car to the shoulder of the road.

I dodged out of the car and fell down the ditch. I finally made my stop at the bottom and dry heaved until bile just as bitter as what I'd seen on the phone spilled out of my mouth.

A hand rubbed my back as I got it out, sobs wracking my chest at the image imprinted in my mind.

Andrew Brindon is in a relationship with Stormy Rodriguez.

CHAPTER THIRTY

I USED the sleeve of my sweater to wipe at my mouth and leaned back in the ditch.

Anika sat beside me and wrapped her arm around my shaking shoulders. "Are you okay?"

Tears streaming down my eyes, I shook my head. "Andrew. He's...dating. Someone else." The words made my stomach turn again, but I swallowed heavily.

"Oh, Skye," Anika breathed, squeezing me just a little tighter.

The sound of the car's engine stopped, but the headlights stayed on, panning out over a dead, empty field.

Brandon crunched down the ditch and came to a stop beside us. "What's going on?"

I drifted in and out of reality as Anika gave him the simplified version.

"That prick," Brandon muttered, and fresh tears found my eyes.

"Hold on," he said. "I think I have something that might help."

What could possibly help? My boyfriend—the guy I'd given up Kellum for, the guy who made me feel like I was good enough as just me—had a girlfriend. Who wasn't me. He hadn't even waited to see what was going on before moving on to someone else.

Brandon landed in the dry grass beside me and handed me a water bottle. "Rinse your mouth out." He said it in a no-nonsense way that had me getting up to my feet and walking away from them so I could clean out my mouth.

I came back and sat down between them with the half-empty water bottle.

He handed me a flask. "Drink."

I raised my eyebrows. "My stomach's already upset."

He shook his head. "It's not for this." He patted my stomach. "It's for this." He tapped my chest, the spot right where my heart used to be.

That was all the prodding I needed. I flipped the

cap open and took a swig. The liquid burned down my throat and settled in my stomach, warming me from the inside out.

"More," he said.

I drank until it didn't burn so much and handed it back.

He stuck it out to Anika. "Want some?"

She gripped the flask. "Eh, why the hell not?"

She drank just as much as I had, coughed, then gave it to Brandon. He stored it in his sweatpants pocket.

Anika sighed and laid back against the incline of the ditch. I reclined beside her, lacing my hands behind my head. It was cool outside, just cool enough I wouldn't have minded having a blanket or something other than my sweats on. But the night was bright, and thousands of stars pinpricked the sky in light shades of yellow, blue, and red.

Brandon laid back beside me, and we all scooted together, using each other's warmth to mingle with the heat from whatever drink Andrew had given us.

Slowly, we started talking. About love, life, college.

"You think high school is going to be so great," I said. "Like you're going to date guys, play sports, go to prom." A sad laugh escaped my chest. "And then you end up laying in a ditch."

Anika nodded. "Why do you think I'm so terrified to date? I mean, it only ends in heartache," she said. "And then what? You go to college, suffer through long distance, and then...get married? It doesn't seem that great to me."

Brandon propped himself on his elbow and looked over at us. "Come on. Tell me you haven't dreamt of some Prince Charming coming in and sweeping you off your feet."

"That's the problem," I said. "I kept waiting and waiting for this perfect guy to come, and then he did, and then..." Fat tears dripped from the corners of my eyes into my ears. "This guy comes and then you realize that he wasn't really Prince Charming. He was just a nice guy—or a guy you thought was nice. And then you realize no matter what you do, no matter how hard you try or how much you do your hair or how sweet your text messages were, it doesn't matter. None of it matters."

"Exactly," Anika said. "Because he's not going to change, even if you give him everything you have."

I glanced over and saw tears rolling down her face as well. I wasn't the only one with a broken heart.

"This is bullshit," Brandon said. "Look at you two. Two of the most beautiful girls I've ever seen. You know how to tell jokes, laugh, dance like hell, and are two of the greatest friends. These guys don't deserve this. They don't deserve the best of you."

If something like that even existed.

Brandon paused. "I have to believe that when you meet the right person, things will just click. It won't be all this tears and heartache and wondering what if crap. It'll be easy, because love—that's easy. You don't question it."

Anika sniffled. "I'm pretty sure my guy like that got hit by a bus."

Despite myself, I laughed. "Or fell off a cliff."

She rolled to her side and put a hand on my arm. "Or ran with the bulls and got stabbed by one of the horns and his guts spilled everywhere."

"Gross." I giggled.

"Totally," Anika said.

Bran huffed and laid back down. "Lightweights."

I wished. I wished I could be light as a feather and drift up into the sky, bathe in the inky darkness and feel little lights swirling around me. But having these two on either side was good enough. For now.

CHAPTER THIRTY-ONE

BRANDON PULLED the car back into McClellan. My buzz was wearing off, my throat hurt, and my eyelids felt scratchy. The clock said it was well past three.

"Hey," Anika said. "We could probably go by Walmart and buy you a phone."

My heart constricted, strangled between the hope of being connected and the fear of confronting Andrew. Of hearing my worst fears confirmed.

"That's okay," I said. "I should probably get home."

I gave them directions to my house, and they parked in the driveway. His headlights illuminated the peeling paint, but at least they couldn't see the chaos inside.

Brandon put the car in park, and I leaned over the front seat to hug Anika. "Thanks for coming. I don't know what I would have done without you guys." I squeezed Bran's shoulder.

"Any time," Anika said. "I think I needed a good cry."

Brandon snorted. "You got one in, alright."

She punched him in the arm. "Hey Skye, you should come to our prom next weekend! Bran will sign you in."

I looked at Bran who was smiling sleepily. "For the record, Anika doesn't need to tell me to ask you out."

"Thanks?"

"So you'll come?" Anika asked.

"Of course!" My face fell. "If my parents will let me go. I'm supposed to be grounded 'til school's out."

Anika frowned. "Well, if you could talk them into it, it would be awesome. I think they're setting up a bowling alley for after prom this year. And you can come get ready at my house," she said. "My parents should be fine with it."

A twinge of jealousy wrenched at my gut. What would it like to have parents who supported friendships that much?

We finished saying goodbye, and I walked into

the house. Thankfully, Mom and Dad were still asleep, and I fell into bed, wishing I could sleep until graduation.

When I woke up the next morning, Andrew was my first thought. I rolled over and moaned. Anika and Bran weren't there to distract me anymore. It was time to deal with the pain and whatever else I was feeling.

Dad was outside, working on starting a garden, and Mom was in the kitchen, balancing the checkbooks and paying bills. She asked me how prom went, and I almost told her about Andrew. Almost.

"It was good," I said.

I grabbed a snack from the fridge and went back to my room. I sat down at my desk and opened my journal. I had a poem dancing around the corners of my mind, and I needed to get it down.

"The Game"
By Skye Hoffner

I want to run and hide and play
*   a game inside my mind.*
*   I'd be the picture-perfect girl,*
*   he'd never leave behind.*
*   We'd kiss into the evening sun,*

hold hands until the dew,
and dream a life of love and joy,
then start our lives anew.
We'd marry under stars so bright,
make love into the day,
then sit together with our cups
and watch our children play.
He'd write me songs,
I'd sit in awe,
cheeks pink with burning love.
And then we'd fall asleep again,
fitting closer than a glove.
I'd never have to ask him if
he knew I was the one,
because no one could question
a love brighter than the sun.

CHAPTER THIRTY-TWO

FOR THE NEXT WEEK, I worked as hard as I could at school and debate and chores at home. Half to keep my parents happy and half to keep Andrew off my mind. On Wednesday, Mom announced she got a bonus from her work—unusually good news. Her and Dad's high spirits from the extra money gave me the courage I needed to ask if I could stay the night at Anika's and go to Roderdale's prom.

Honestly, I hadn't been expecting much. I was supposed to be grounded for another three weeks, but they surprised me by saying yes. They said they wanted to use the bonus to get out of town on a vacation by themselves, so it worked out.

I was trying to tell myself that it was positive, but

I had a hard time getting myself to smile about anything. I missed Andrew more than I could put into words. He'd been my boyfriend, my best friend, and the only person I could really count on to be there for me, if only on the phone. But now he was worse than a stranger. I didn't want to hear from him, didn't want to know how he and what's-her-name started dating or listen to any excuses.

On Saturday, my parents left for their mini vacation a few hours before Anika was coming to pick me up. Usually, I'd get on the computer and check Facebook with them gone. This time, I took a nap. I almost didn't want to get up to go to Roderdale, but I didn't have a way of calling to cancel.

Anika picked me up in her mom's suburban a few hours before the prom, and when we arrived at her house, we got busy doing each other's hair and makeup. We didn't talk about Andrew, but she told me about working cattle with Kyle Rayford, a really good-looking guy from her school and her neighbor— if you counted someone who lived two miles away as a neighbor.

He would have been perfect for her, but he'd been dating the same girl for about a year. "When is he going to break up with Melissa?" I asked.

Anika sighed. "Not soon enough. She's such a jerk."

I chewed on my lip, thinking about a different jerk. "Do you think it's going to be awkward with James there?"

She shrugged. "I mean, you'll be with Bran and me. And Rhett and Savannah will be there, so you'll know people. Plus, if he gives you any trouble"—she slapped a fist against her open palm—"I'll take care of him."

"You sure?"

She put on a mobster accent. "You wants me to whack him for ya?"

And for the first time since the week before, I laughed. "Please."

From upstairs, Anika's mom shouted, "Brandon's here!"

The sound of his footsteps plodding down the stairs came first, and then he came to stand with us.

"Looking good!" he said and winked at us.

I knew he was joking because I was still wearing a paint-stained pair of shorts and one of Anika's dad's old button-up shirts.

"You too," I said, but much less sarcastically.

Bran was actually cute, but in a little brother kind of way.

"Do a spin," Anika ordered.

He put his toe down on the carpet and twisted around.

"Nice," she said, nodding her approval.

He smiled, blushing a little bit, but she was already looking back at my hair.

On the way to the dance, I borrowed a pocket mirror from Anika to make sure my makeup was looking good... James might not cause me any trouble, but after my second failed relationship, thanks to my parents, I wanted him to see me at my best. To see what he was missing.

Bran pulled into the parking lot and came to the other side of the car to open the door for both of us. He stuck his arm out, and I looped mine through his, feeling less like broken Skye and more like the girl I'd been before.

We walked into the school together for the prom supper. We were there a little later than everyone else, so the food was already being served when we sat down.

Anika spread a napkin over her lap, then her jaw dropped. "Oh my God, Skye."

"What?" I looked her over. Was something wrong?

"Don't look," she whispered, "but James is here with someone…"

Of course he had a date. Why wouldn't he? Not that knowing that made it any easier to deal with. "Who?"

She shook her head.

I couldn't not look. I searched the room for him and saw him sitting next to Kylie. The girl I used to trust with all my secrets. The girl who let me stay over and ate ice cream with me as I sobbed about James breaking up with me.

They were holding hands, and James had his lips near her ear, whispering something that made her giggle. She looked so stunning I wanted to cry. Her dress must have cost more than twice what mine had brand new.

My heart hurt like the knife Kylie'd stabbed into my back had finally reached all the way through to finish me off.

"You're better off without him," Anika said. "He's been so full of himself just because he got a college deal."

"College deal?"

"You didn't hear?" Bran asked. "Everyone's been going crazy over it."

Anika rolled her eyes. "He signed to play basketball at Upton. Full ride."

"Of course he did," I muttered, tasting acid.

"Don't worry about it." Bran patted me on the
shoulder. "You're way better off without him."

"One hundred percent," Anika said.

For whatever reason, that didn't make me feel
any better. I forced myself to eat supper and act like
nothing was wrong. James and I'd been broken up
for a year—never even dated, really, and we'd only
kissed once. So why did breathing hurt so badly?

Bran, Anika, and I walked through promenade as
a threesome and then went to the dance. I got the first
slow song with Brandon, so Anika got the second.

While they took the floor, I sat along the edge of
the gym, watching James and Kylie spinning much
too close. Even though it hurt, I couldn't look away.

Rhett sat down next to me. "Hey, Skye."

"Hey," I said, working to put a smile on my face,
and gave him a hug. "You look great."

"Speak for yourself," he said. "Brandon's a lucky
guy."

I rolled my eyes. "He just signed me in."

He put his hand up and leaned forward like he
was whispering. "I knew that."

"Where's Savannah?" I asked. "I didn't see you guys at the supper."

I looked around the dark gym and caught sight of her dancing with another guy from Roderdale. One of Rhett's friends, I thought.

"We had supper at my house with Vox's and Har's dates," he said. "Steaks and potatoes."

"That sounds good."

He laughed. "I thought so. Want to dance?"

There was only about a minute of the song left, but I was glad he'd saved me from sitting by myself watching my former best friend danced with my ex-boyfriend.

After the song ended, I caught Kylie looking at me. My mind froze, caught in this mess. She stepped toward me, and I made a beeline for the bathroom. I couldn't handle this. Couldn't let her see me fall apart.

She knew how much I liked him. We'd talked about him at almost every sleepover the year before. She'd comforted me when I was heartbroken about him calling it quits. Sure, she'd gone over to Shelby's side this year, but this was a far worse betrayal than that.

I locked myself in a stall, lifting the bottom of my dress up around my waist before sitting down.

"Skye?"

I folded over so my head was on my knees, keeping my eyes squeezed shut so tears wouldn't fall and ruin my makeup. "Hey, Kylie."

Her voice sounded tentative, nervous. "I didn't know you were coming to the prom here."

My breath came out ragged, even though I fought to keep it even. "I came with Brandon and Anika."

"Look, I was gonna ask you if it was okay for me to come with James, but he said that you guys were fine, and..." Her sentence trailed off.

We were *not* fine. *He* was fine, because he broke up with me and now he got to go to prom with someone even better. The upgraded version of the McClellan girl.

"You know him better than I do," I said over the tightness in my throat. I couldn't do this, couldn't break down. That would mean she'd won, that Shelby had won. "Are you having a good time?"

"Yeah." She paused for a second. "I'll see you out there?"

"See you out there."

Her heels clacked against the tile, and the door banged shut behind her. A huge whoosh of breath I'd been holding escaped my mouth. My chest deflated, like I could have dissolved into a pile of taffeta and mascara, right there on the bathroom floor.

Kylie wasn't my friend. She never had been.

CHAPTER THIRTY-THREE

AT HOME the day before state, it was one of those rare nights when Dad cooked. He made chicken fried steak and mashed potatoes, and everyone seemed to be in a good mood except for me.

I tried to laugh and joke and pay attention when they talked about their hotel stay and the handsy couples' masseuse, but I couldn't. It was a feat just to get the food into my mouth.

Mom got up from the table, and on her way to the living room, she said, "Skye, can you do the dishes?"

"I need to pack a bag for state." That was partially true. Really, I *hated* doing dishes. We didn't have a dishwasher, so I would have to do it all by hand. Plus, Mom and Dad usually let the dishes go, so there was already a giant stack of plates crusted with food sitting in the sink.

"Just do the dishes," Dad said.

So he cooked supper one night, and I had to do several days' worth of dishes? Dad never had to do any chores around the house because he made the money. At least, that's what he said when he and Mom fought about it late at night. But I was too tired to argue.

I pushed my chair back and started cleaning up the mess.

When most of the dishes were done, I reached into dirty water to see what was left in the bottom of the sink. My finger stung with a sharp pain. A knife hiding under the water. The pain in my finger blended with the pain in my heart, and tears dripped down my cheeks, even though I did everything I could do blink through them and shove them down.

What if I'd cut myself on purpose?

The thought came like someone else had whispered it in my ear, and I jumped back from the sink, too afraid to keep drying. Liz used to cut, and I'd never understood it before now.

I looked over into the living room. Mom and Dad were already watching TV. Taking a deep breath, I dried my hands off on a rag. My finger left a bright red streak of blood.

I reached my arm up to wipe my eyes on my sleeve. "Mom? Dad?"

Mom glanced toward me. "Yeah?"

Hearing, rather than feeling, my pulse, I walked into the living room and edged onto the couch with Mom. "I need to talk to you guys."

"Okay," Mom said, angling her knees slightly so she was facing me.

Dad looked at us from the recliner, but he left the TV on. Some guys in a forest were trying to start a fire so they could cook some kind of bug. I'd rather eat it than have this conversation.

I closed my eyes against the screen and against the fear I felt. They probably wouldn't understand, but I had to try... "I'm really depressed."

"Why do you say that?" Mom asked.

I opened my eyes to see disbelief plain on her face. Dad picked at his thumbnail, avoiding eye contact.

"I—" I wanted to tell them how sad I'd felt since volleyball season, how the only thing keeping me going was avoiding everyone and focusing on school, how excluded I'd felt when Shelby's mom hadn't added me to the "100 Things To Be Thankful For" list, or how pathetic I felt that even my older sister wasn't speaking to me anymore. I wanted to tell them how talking with Andrew had brightened my days, given me hope, but even that was gone now. And it all sounded so trivial. So, I started with the thing that scared me most. "When I was trying to wash the knives, I thought about using it on myself."

I looked down at the couch's worn-out upholstery and tried not to cry again.

"You're kidding," Mom said, incredulous. "We've seen depressed—went through hell with Liz—and you're nowhere near as bad as she was."

Her words might as well have wrapped shackles around my ankles and held me upside down for how backwards this whole thing felt.

"Mom, I've been feeling this way for a long time. Ever since volleyball, and especially since I hurt my knee—"

Mom got up from the couch and towered over me, her hands on her hips. "Just because you haven't had as much attention from your knee as you thought you would doesn't mean you need to invent another problem."

Dad's voice took on that dismissive tone that said *I don't care about you* even more clearly than his words did. "She's just trying to get out of doing the dishes."

"Are you kidding?" Angry tears stung my eyes, and I hated the shakiness that entered my voice. "I come to you after *months* of dealing with this, and you tell me I'm trying to get attention?"

"Shut up," Dad barked.

But I couldn't. "Your daughter's here with a knife thinking she's going to cut herself, and all you care about is whether the dishes get done or not?"

"Stop it right now," Mom said.

"What? Stop talking about my feelings?" I yelled, standing up from the couch. "Do I have to mutilate myself like Liz before you start caring?"

Dad snapped the footrest back on the recliner. "Shut the hell up, and do the God damn dishes."

I faded back until my calves hit the couch, afraid of what he might do.

He stumbled through the hallway, and their bedroom door slammed so loudly it rattled the windowpanes. Mom left the living room, too, going into the bathroom.

When I heard the shower turn on, I got up, went to the kitchen, and finished doing the dishes...but I left the knives in the sink.

CHAPTER THIRTY-FOUR

MRS. GRADY BROUGHT music for the trip to state debate. Surprisingly, I didn't hear the song "Respect" one single time. She liked a variety of genres, most of them enjoyable. I had my speeches printed out and was attempting to look them over, listen to the music, and take in what the others were talking about all at the same time.

Reese, Mr. Yen, and Mrs. Grady had been trading corny jokes for the last half hour.

Reese leaned forward. "What goes 'bow wow tick tock'?"

"What?" Mrs. Grady played along this time.

"A watchdog!" Reese burst out in laughter so contagious even I joined in.

Reese suddenly quieted and motioned us to do

the same. "What happens when you don't pay your exorcist?" he began.

Mrs. Grady asked, "What?"

"You get repossessed!"

Mr. Yen belted out a loud, "HA! HA! HA!"

"Oh, Reese." Mrs. Grady wiped at her eyes.

I forced a smile, but I couldn't get my mind off the whirlwind day about to come. Tomorrow, I'd be performing in the biggest competition of my life and coming face-to-face with the guy who tore my heart in shreds until it looked like mangled confetti. I'd been through a lot, but this? This was a whole new level.

Homework used to distract me from Shelby. Debate distracted me from my knee injury. Andrew distracted me from my crumbling life. But now I had nothing to distract me from Andrew.

Hanging out with Mr. Yen, Mrs. Grady, and Reese was better anyway. At least, that's what I tried to tell myself. We went out and ate—paid for by the school—then Mr. Yen drove us to the mall. Mrs. Grady opted to watch over Reese, and Mr. Yen let me browse on my own as long as I told him where I was going and checked in with him before switching stores. He said the benches were calling his name.

Thankfully, I was well hidden when I caught

sight of Andrew walking into the same store as me—
an athletic shop. He was with another girl and a guy
from his team. They were talking animatedly and
totally oblivious to me. For now.

I dodged behind a rack of basketballs. Don't see
me. Please don't see me.

Their voices became more coherent as they
walked closer to my hiding spot. Peeking over the
orange balls, I checked to make sure the coast was
clear. Andrew was glancing through a rack of shirts.
He looked painfully good—short, light brown hair,
bright pink cheeks, blue eyes softer than an old t-
shirt. But the worst part? He looked like I wasn't on
his mind at all.

Before he could see me, I got up and dashed
between clothing racks and out of the store. I walked
straight to the benches where Mr. Yen sat with his
nose in a book and told him I was ready to go. With
one call to Mrs. Grady, we were on our way to the
hotel.

Mr. Yen and Reese had a room together, and that
meant Mrs. Grady and I were in the same room.

She was using the bathroom, but I needed a
shower to relax. My dress clothes were already hung
up, so I didn't have to worry about that. I'd finished
my homework somewhere between bow wow tick

tock and a joke about a priest. I wouldn't dare pull out my journal for fear Mrs. Grady would catch a glance at some of its contents.

The bathroom door opened, and Mrs. Grady came out, toweling her hair. I picked up my pajamas to bring in the bathroom with me.

"Hey, Skye?" She sat on her bed. "Can I ask you something?"

My tongue caught in my mouth for a second. I didn't know why I felt so nervous to talk to her... maybe her cautious tone of voice.

"Sure." I smoothed my pajama pants where they lay over my arm.

"What's been going on at school?"

"What do you mean?" I asked, confused.

My grades had been as good as ever, and I'd been respectful in class. Plus, I'd been doing such a good job at acting like I was alright that my own parents didn't believe me when I told them I felt depressed.

She looked down at her lap. "Well, you've been rather withdrawn for the last few months, and so much of your poetry is about hopelessness..." She lifted her gaze to meet mine, but I couldn't look her in the eyes. "Is it something going on at home?"

When wasn't something going on at home? If Mom and Dad weren't fighting, it was only a question of when they would start again. I was grounded until the end of the schoolyear. To top it off, I had to use every bit of my strength to get out of bed in the morning because I dreaded going to school each day. Oh, and of course there was the fact that the one guy I was in love with had chosen someone else over me. I was one step away from falling into a black tar pit I didn't have a chance of crawling my way out of.

But it had all started somewhere. "Just that thing with Shelby."

She put the towel down. "What's going on with you two?"

"She's been...bullying me...like she told people not to invite me to this thing after the bonfire and she basically turned everyone in the school against me." It sounded ridiculous even as I said it, but it was the truth.

"You know, when I was in high school, I was bullied too."

I raised my eyebrows. Mrs. Grady was easily one of the most well-liked, charismatic teachers at McClellan.

"I'm serious. One time this girl put a dead bird in my locker."

"You're kidding."

For a moment, her lips turned down, but she

quickly recovered and started braiding her frizzing hair. "Another time, someone put a list on the outside of my locker and it had two categories: guys Fran wants, and guys Fran can get. Guess which side of the list was blank."

The fan in the bathroom was the only sound between us. I couldn't find anything to say, couldn't look at her, couldn't let her see the tears that always seemed prepped and ready to go.

"It gets better," she said.

I looked at her, searching her face for some kind of honesty. "Does it?"

"It has to."

CHAPTER THIRTY-FIVE

7:33 AM, the morning of state. That's when I saw Andrew, his perfectly pressed suit, the small American flag pinned on his lapel.

Our eyes met for the briefest of moments, and I pretended to watch Mr. Yen at the registration table.

Then he did a double take. "Skye?"

I kept my head down. Turning toward Mrs. Grady, I said, "Bathroom."

I ducked between students, walked past the restrooms, and turned down an empty hallway. The second I got far enough away for the morning chatter to become white noise, I slumped down against a wall. With my eyes closed, I knit my fingers through my curly hair until they stuck. I made fists and pulled like I could rip the tension away from my scalp.

After minutes in that position, I opened my folder and started going through my speech.

More often than I should have, I thought of Andrew. Most of all, I wanted to know what he'd thought when he couldn't get a hold of me. How he went from "I want to date you" to *in a relationship with Stormy Rodriguez.*

I swallowed my heartache, stored it in the vault that kept my life's most painful questions. That vault was the only thing that got me out of the hallway and back to my team. Back to what I came here to do.

My first round went well, but round two's performance was even better. In round three, I really caught my stride, giving my best speech of the season.

When I finished performing, I paced in front of the wall where they would be posting the results. Twelve students from every event would be chosen to compete in semifinals, and I couldn't stand the thought of not being one of them.

"Let's see how you did."

I looked over to see Mr. Yen. He was sporting a small, excited smile as he leaned closer so only I could hear him. "It's going to be close."

More than fifty students, parents, and coaches had crowded around us and the wall, waiting to see the lucky few whose season would continue. A robust woman came forward with several large sheets of paper in her hands, trailed by more students trying to sneak a glance at the results.

Mentally crossing my fingers, I checked the sheet with "INFORMATIVE" written across the top. In someone's loopy handwriting, four rows down, I saw my name: Skye Hoffner.

"No way."

Mr. Yen squeezed my shoulder. "Good job, kid."

Mrs. Grady sidled between two students, scanning the results. "Skye, did you..." Stopping next to me, her gaze landed on the results, and her mouth split into a wide smile. "Yes! That's awesome!"

Mrs. Grady pulled me into a hug, dancing back and forth so her high heels clacked against the tile.

Mr. Yen grinned between the two of us. "I'm going to go look at the judges' comments again. Go wait at our table until I come find you."

"Okay," I said, suddenly feeling the pressure of semifinals and the crush of people around me. I needed to get somewhere I could take a breath.

Mrs. Grady gave me another excited hug. "I have

to go judge, but keep up the good work. I'm rooting for you."

"Thank you."

She dodged through the crowd, and I looked at the sheet one more time, following the pattern of my name with my eyes.

This was really happening.

I tore myself away to go back to the table with my things. I sat down, resting my head in my hands. In the blackness of my closed eyes, I counted down from ten, fighting the flood of nerves and excitement pooling into an ocean of unease in my stomach.

"Skye. Hey, Skye!"

I'd know that voice anywhere. I turned around to see Andrew coming my way. My stomach, heart, everything inside of me melted into a pile of mush. He was smiling, like he was most of the time, and walked closer to my table, stopping to stand next to me. Up close, I could see his smile was a little hurt, a little guarded.

"Andrew..." I looked down at my speech. It hurt how much I wanted to run my fingers over his lips, fall into his arms and wish away all our problems. But I couldn't. "What happened?"

His real feelings—those he hid below the surface —passed over his eyes. "Skye, I—"

A hand rested on my shoulder, and I looked up to see Reese staring hard at Andrew.

Andrew lifted his chin, thinly veiling his confusion.

"I think you better go." Reese's voice was hard in a way I hadn't heard it before. "There'll be time after finals."

Andrew frowned, one side of his mouth dropping more than the other, but he managed to smile at me. "Good luck, Skye."

"Good luck," I breathed.

Reese kept his hand on my shoulder until Andrew had disappeared behind the other students, then he faced me, putting both hands on my shoulders. "You okay?"

I took a deep breath, trying to shake the burning behind my eyes. Mostly, I felt tired. Tired from the trip. Tired from the day. Tired of not being good enough. "I'm fine." Whatever that meant.

"Look." Reese dipped his knees so we were eye level. "You haven't practiced all these hours, dedicated all your time to this, to let some asshole swoop in and ruin it for you at the last minute, okay?"

I nodded, eyes burning.

"Good. Listen to me." His eyes searched mine. "Mr. Yen's going to give you some last-minute comments from the judges. Don't let them throw you off. If you weren't good, you wouldn't be here. Just practice your speech, be confident in the fact that you know more about this subject than anyone here, and smile. You'll do great."

My lips lifted on their own, and I wiped at my eyes, careful not to mess up my mascara. "Thanks, Shiloh."

He nodded. "Anytime, Hoffner."

I ran through my speech once more before Mr. Yen came back with comments scribbled on a notepad. They were small tweaks, like moving more purposely or keeping eye contact.

"You're going to do great," he said, setting the legal pad on the table. "Between you and Reese, I think we can get some medals today."

In a trance induced by weeks of practice and routine, I went to perform. On the way to the room, my footsteps echoed my heartbeat. I said a small, clumsy prayer, reminded myself of what Reese had said, and entered the room to give what could be my last speech of the season.

Once I was done, all I had to do was wait.

Though I wanted to make it to finals, I doubted I would. Mr. Yen told me it was close getting into semifinals, meaning it would be nearly impossible to make it further in the competition. Top six in Texas? Yeah right.

Back in the cafeteria, the semifinal postings were torn down, and the finals participants announced in writing on similar sheets of paper.

Instead of looking toward the papers, I watched everyone else. Kids everywhere looked anxiously at the wall. Some grinned triumphantly at the sheets. Others tried to fake a smile and shrugged at their friends. The more involved ones cried.

I searched for Andrew. He walked up to the sheets and smiled as wide as the time I'd told him I'd be his girlfriend.

"I made it!" he called over his shoulder to his coach.

Mr. Yen found me amongst the students. "I'm going to have to go help in the tab room," he said over the commotion, "but I want to give you some advice before you go to perform."

"What?"

"What do you mean?"

"I'm going to perform?"

"Right." He furrowed his eyebrows and nodded slowly. "You are going to perform, right?"

"Wait..." I finally looked over at the wall, and

underneath Informative, there was my name. My throat felt tight. "I made it?"

He grinned. "You made it. Now let me give you some advice." He waved at me to follow him and started walking out of the cafeteria. "You need to speak more forcefully. Make your movements purposeful."

We stopped in front of the school's office, and inside, I saw adults milling about the room. Judges and coaches, I guessed, gathering notes, making plans.

The fact that I made it to the final round hit me like the stream of a warm shower after a hard work-out. "I made it?"

Grinning, he tucked his legal pad under his right arm and gave me a side hug with his left. "Have fun, kid. Top six in the state ain't too shabby."

I went back to the lunchroom where Reese sat at the table with his mom. She looked so beautiful and young with her bouncy blond hair and deep plum pantsuit. I felt inferior just standing across from them—Reese in a brand name suit and his mom looking like she stepped out of the White House for a first lady's luncheon.

"Mrs. Shiloh," I said, surprised. I hadn't seen her earlier that morning. "How are you?"

"I'm wonderful, thank you. Took off work just in time, apparently."

Swallowing those insecure feelings, I looked directly at Reese. "You made it?"

He broke out in a grin. "Looks like we both did."

I nodded, matching his smile.

"Way to go, Hoffner."

Feeling the heat in my cheeks as his mom closely watched our exchange, I said. "Thanks. I guess I better start practicing."

He dipped his head and got back to flipping through his stack of research. Mrs. Shiloh had already redirected her attention to a sleek looking smart phone.

There was no way I'd find any peace in the lunch room, so I went back to the same hallway from that morning and found a corner to practice in. All that was on my mind was my speech. It had to be.

Halfway through my run-through, I heard someone cough behind me.

A short boy with messy brown hair sat cross-legged a few feet away, staring intently up at me. His hands were folded neatly under his chin and his brown eyes were magnified by thick, wire-rimmed glasses.

"What are you doing?" I asked in disbelief.

He smiled sweetly. "Watching you," he said, his nasally voice saturated with admiration.

Was he trying to distract me before finals?

I narrowed my eyes. "Are you in informative?"

He shook his head quickly. "Extemp."

"Okay..." I didn't know what to make of this. So, I handled the situation the way I'd dealt with every other problem throughout the year: I ignored it. I turned back to the wall and continued practicing my speech where I'd left off.

Right after the conclusion, he stood up and took off.

CHAPTER THIRTY-SIX

I HEARD him before I saw him—Andrew called my name. "Skye?"

I looked over my shoulder and contorted my face into a smile. "Yeah?"

Smiling used to come so easily around him. Now, it felt wrong. The false warmth on my face didn't even hold a candle to the ice in my chest.

"How are you?" His tone was normal, but his face expressed a mingled look of concern and regret.

I hated it.

"Fine," I replied.

"Let's go walk around," he suggested.

"Okay." I stood up from my chair.

I led, with Andrew always following a step behind like a puppy with its head down and tail between its legs. The guilty way he walked made me feel even worse. He knew he'd cheated on me. There was no way this could be a misunderstanding. But how could someone who hurt me so much still hold my heart under such a firm grasp?

I stopped at a stairwell on the opposite end of the school and sat down, leaving enough room for him to sit beside me.

The feeling from prom night came back times ten. I wanted to cry. I wanted to scream. I wanted to run without stopping. My body felt like a cage. My knee was weak and useless. Everything about me was weak and useless. Maybe that was why Andrew took off when he had the chance.

He settled in beside me, close enough to touch.

"Andrew, I..." but I couldn't figure out what I wanted to say, so I didn't say anything.

He rubbed his hand over his face. "What happened? Why'd you stop talking to me?" The hurt came through in his voice. "Every time I called, it went straight to voicemail, and then it said your number was disconnected."

"My parents broke my phone!" I hissed. "I couldn't talk to you, so I had Reese message you, and you never replied."

He looked confused.

"They broke it," I said. "Like, in half."

He shook his head, eyebrows knitting together. "I know what broken means. He never messaged me."

I frowned. "Yes, he did. He showed me the message."

"Well, I never got it! I've been worried sick—wondering if something happened to you or if I'd done something wrong, and I had no idea who to call or what to ask, and I couldn't drive there."

"You were worried?" I asked, disbelief plain in my tone.

A muscle in Andrew's cheek tensed and relaxed. "I thought about you all the time. I still do."

My heart battled between what he was saying and the truth. "No, you don't."

He could say anything he wanted, but that didn't make it true. No matter how much I wanted it to be true, that didn't make it true. I knew Reese had sent the message, and Andrew's new relationship status more than proved he hadn't been that concerned.

"Can you just listen to me?" he snapped.

My head jerked back at the force of his words.

"I liked you," he said, finally looking at me, but he wasn't smiling. His mouth turned down at the corners and his eyes blazed, two blue flames. "At first I thought it wouldn't be anything, because everyone's always told me high school relationships don't go anywhere, but then I got to know you. I always wanted to see your pretty blue eyes and hear that amazing laugh of yours. And you weren't just my girlfriend. You were my best friend... When you stopped talking to me, I had no idea what to do."

I turned away, blinking fast. I would not cry in front of Andrew. Wouldn't make myself more pathetic than I already was.

"Say something," he begged.

I opened my eyes, and all of my painful thoughts broke through the floodgates of my eyelids. "What are we?"

He paused, biting the inside of his cheek. "You can't be in a relationship with someone you can't even talk to."

I stood up and mustered all the energy I had left to look him in the eyes.

This was my life, and I didn't need a guy who couldn't make up his mind, who got a new girlfriend and didn't apologize for it.

And I would be fine. I knew I would be fine, because I'd always been. I'd made it through every single worst day of my life, and here I was. Standing. On my own. And sometimes, that had to be enough.

"You're right," I said. "We shouldn't be anything more than friends."

With an almost imperceptible waver in his voice, he said, "Good. I couldn't take losing you as a friend too."

CHAPTER THIRTY-SEVEN

I GRIPPED the armrests of my auditorium chair. "What if I get sixth?"

Mrs. Grady was sitting on my right and Mr. Yen to my left. Reese sat behind us with his Mom because he felt like there was "too much anxiety" in our row. Well, he was right—annoyingly so.

"You made it to finals," Mrs. Grady tried to comfort me. "You're top six in the entire state. That's pretty impressive."

A sly smile twisted Mr. Yen's lips. "You didn't get sixth."

"Great, fifth place." Optimism was clearly my forte.

A small group of people moved onto the stage and started laying out flashing medals on a table.

"Hurry up," I muttered. I wanted to get my medal, get out of there, and sleep until the last day of school when I'd be ungrounded. One week left.

Mrs. Grady laughed "If you keep this up, Murphy's Law states informative will be called last."

"Great."

"It'll be fine," Mr. Yen said.

That didn't help. My stomach had reshaped itself into an origami swan by the time the woman in charge of the meet took the stage.

As Mrs. Grady—and Murphy's Law—predicted, my event was called last. The only event I actually listened to, besides my own, was Extemp—Andrew and Reese were both in that. And the weird little guy who'd watched me practicing. Did I have a type?

Andrew and Reese stood as far apart from each other on the stage as they could. Seeing Andrew up there, his calm demeanor, his soft smile under stage lights...it hurt. But I reminded myself I'd be okay, no matter what, no matter who was in or out of my life.

Andrew placed sixth. I clapped supportively for him. I didn't hate him. Just saw him as who he was—a guy who used to be my sun, falling over a horizon in my life.

Contestants stepped off the stage until the only

two left standing were Reese and my little admirer from before. He rocked forward and backward with his hands folded in front of him.

The woman called out Reese's name for second place, and my breath stalled. The little guy had a grin so wide it caught the stage lights and reflected the silver of his braces. First place.

At last, I took the stage with five other kids. Up there, the stage lights felt more like the ones from the operating room. I glanced down the row of my competitors. Some looked as nervous as I did. Others seemed totally at ease.

Mr. Yen hadn't lied: I didn't get sixth place. The woman called fifth place in her grating voice, and I took a step toward the medal, but realized my name hadn't been called. Places ticked off until it was only me and one other girl on the stage.

First place? No way. I couldn't even bring myself to imagine my knee injury had bought me a gold medal.

"In second place, Skye Hoffner from McClellan High School."

There was a smattering of polite applause, and I found myself grinning and shaking someone's hand and holding a small silver medal—a representation of my hard work. Of the fact that I'd turned my pain into something meaningful.

I ran my thumb over the engraved surface of the silver medal. Definitely not sixth place.

CHAPTER THIRTY-EIGHT

AT HOME, I found Mom and Dad in the living room.

"How'd it go?" Mom asked.

Dad actually twisted around in his recliner to hear my answer.

Holding up my silver medal, I said, "I got second in informative!"

"Wow, that's great," Mom said and got up to give me a hug. She smelled like wine and cleaning supplies.

"Good job, squirt," Dad chimed in.

"Thanks." I let go of Mom and stepped back to show her the medal.

She smiled as she examined the best trophy I'd ever won. Then, she handed it to Dad.

"So what was your speech about again?" he asked, still looking at the design on the front.

I fought back my disappointment that he didn't even know. "ACL injuries."

"She's been doing that spe—" Mom started, but Dad talked over her.

"Well, I guess you're an expert in that by now."

I sat in the living room with my parents and talked with them for the longest we'd spoken amicably in months. Granted, it was mostly Dad telling stories about when he was in high school and Mom asking me questions about things she would know if we ever talked, but it was better than nothing.

They left me alone after that, and I had time to go to my room and relax. I fell into bed and closed my eyes, but all I could see was Andrew's face.

I pictured it in fine detail—how his long eyelashes were almost straight. Or how he talked a little more out of one side of his mouth than the other. Or the way his eyes turned down when he said he couldn't imagine me not being his friend.

I opened my eyes and caught sight of my prom dress hanging in my closet, a reminder of everything that went wrong for us.

Gloomy thoughts clung to me, threatening to

send me spiraling. But this time, the pain seemed more bearable than before because at least I'd seen the light. At least I knew I could claw my way out.

But there was something I needed to do first. I went to my desk and pulled out a fresh sheet of paper.

Dear Andrew,

I love you. I said it: I love you. I know you'll say something like "we're just in high school," and I suppose that would be the sensible thing to say. But I don't care how old I am, and I sure as hell don't care how long I've known you. I know what's in my heart.

I also wanted you to know how much I ~~need~~ needed you. You didn't know it, but when you stepped into my life, everything was falling apart. I'd lost all of the friends I thought I had, I had an injury that derailed my entire future, and I had terrible self-esteem. You were the only thing that kept me going. Your amazing smile and heartfelt compliments, and especially our conversations, were the only things I had to look forward to. You made me believe someone could see the good in me when everything else in my life pointed out my flaws.

All of those negative feelings you dulled came

back times ten when you picked that other girl. Whoever she is. I don't think you realized how hard it was for me to not just lose an amazing guy, but also someone I relied on to be my sunshine. Even though those times are over, I still appreciate all you did for me—whether you knew what you were doing or not.

I don't know what will happen between us in the future. You and I could easily date for a long time after high school. We're compatible...attracted to each other in a way I can't even explain. Even after everything.

But part of this letter is simply admitting I don't know where life will lead me, or us, or if there will even be an "us." I don't even know if I want there to be an "us" again, no matter how much I still love you.

I do know one thing for sure: you are one of the best guys out there. You saved my life. Someday, you will make someone the happiest girl in the world, and I'll be happy for you even if she isn't me.

Good luck, Andrew.

Love,

Skye Hoffner

. . .

I set the pen down and gazed at the page. Andrew couldn't see this letter. It was me—raw, vulnerable in a way I hadn't been with anyone before.

I went into the kitchen and walked past where Mom stood near the microwave, popcorn crackling inside. Her head swiveled, watching me as I walked to the junk drawer and pulled it open.

"What are you looking for?" she asked, leaning against the counter and folding her arms over her chest.

"Nothing," I lied, pushing around the drawer's messy contents. Finally, I found a lighter and tucked it in my waistband. "I'm going to go for a walk. Unwind."

"Okay."

With the letter in my hand and the lighter hidden, I marched outside. Warm wind brushed over my cheeks, through my hair, and it felt good, cleansing. I kept walking until our house light was a pinprick behind me. And then I sat down.

After settling onto the gravel, I held the note at eyelevel, using light from the lighter to read it one more time.

It's almost over, I told myself. It was now or never.

I shifted to my knees, feeling rocks press into my

shins through my sweatpants. Leaning back on my heels, I positioned the lighter in my right hand and the letter in my left. The lighter started easily, and I held it at the edge of the page, right below my name. Flames quickly took to the sheet, replacing all of my words and feelings.

As a black line of ash spread up the letter, I wondered what it would feel like if I were to burn in the flames too. I imagined them licking over my body, the fiery pain overcoming my mental anguish.

The flame stung my fingers, and I dropped it, watching the black scraps of ash float through the air.

As they drifted away into the darkness, I felt a peace I hadn't felt in a very, very long time.

CHAPTER THIRTY-NINE

MOM AND DAD gave me my keys back on the last day of school, telling me they were proud of how I'd handled my punishment. I was surprised, but I wasn't about to question it.

I drove into school, ready for the day, ready for summer.

In weights, Coach Rokey had us clean the weight room on the last day of school. Kellum, Coach Rokey, and I were on our own, talking while we sanitized a row of dumbbells.

"So," Rokey said, "where are you thinking for college?"

"I'm not sure." I replied, dropping a newly cleaned weight on the rack. "I think I want to study counseling, though. Maybe minor in English."

"English?" Kellum looked to me, his dark eyebrows furrowing. "I hate that class."

"Good for you," I teased.

He stuck his tongue out at me.

I couldn't help but laugh at that. Even making a goofy face, Kellum was amazingly handsome. My stomach swooped at the attention, at the memory of my fish, Wattner, sitting on my dresser. Remembering why I'd turned Kellum down sent a shock of pain through my chest. I missed Andrew as a boyfriend, but mostly as a friend.

Instead of cleaning my locker out after school, I went to the bank and withdrew money from my savings account. Then I went to the store and bought a cheap smart phone with a plan that had unlimited data and texting.

In the store's parking lot, I activated the phone and typed out a text.

Me: Hey Anika. It's Skye. Finally got a phone! :D

Then I logged onto Facebook and wrote a message to Andrew. It didn't feel quite right, but I sent it anyway.

Me: Hey. I got a new number. Let me know if you want it.

I went out that night for the first time in a long time. Anika had invited me to a party one of the seniors at Roderdale was having, and I was really excited to see her. My parents even agreed to let me go and said I could stay the night with Anika.

I met Anika at her house, and we took her mom's Suburban to the party. She drove us way out into the country and parked in front of an enormous shop building near a pretty clapboard house.

"So, whose place is this again?" I asked.

"Vox's," she said. "Rhett's friend."

The anxious anticipation I felt at going to a party amplified. Savannah and Rhett had broken up after prom. I didn't know what happened, but she hadn't talked to me about it. That meant Rhett was single, and if his reputation pre-Savannah was anything to go by, it wouldn't take him long to find another girl.

Anika parked behind what looked like a brand-new pickup, its silver paint reflecting the orange, dusky light.

She pulled her spaghetti strap back up her shoulder. "Ready?"

Not sure, I nodded.

She got out, and I followed her to the shop. Country music poured out of the open garage door, and I heard people chattering before I got around the vehicles to see them.

There weren't too many people there, and it was

mostly guys. I recognized most of them from sports, so at least I wasn't a total stranger. I had been worried James would be there, but luckily, I didn't see him in the mix.

I did see Vox reaching into a cooler and passing cans of light beer around. Anika's neighbor, Kyle, was in a one-armed embrace with his girlfriend, Melissa.

Anika went ahead of me. "Hey Vox, pass me one?"

"Sure thing."

"Hey, Skye." Rhett came to stand close enough for me to smell his cologne and see the color under his tan cheeks. "Haven't seen you in a while."

I thanked myself for taking the time to look nice and do my makeup. "It's only been a few weeks."

"Forever," he said, reaching out to hug me.

I laughed into his chest. "It's good to see you too."

He held on for a moment and then released me. "Wanna beer?"

I smiled and tried to play it cool. "Maybe later."

"Awesome." He smiled and sauntered off to another group of people.

I tucked my hands into my pockets and tried not to look awkward while I waited for Anika, who stood chatting with Kyle. The soft purr of an engine came from further down the gravel drive, and a small white car pulled away from the shop. That must have been his girlfriend.

Vox came over and slung one of his meaty arms around my shoulders. "How are ya, Skye?"

"Oh, pretty good." I smiled at him as he took a swig from the drink he was holding. We weren't really friends, but close enough, I guessed.

He swayed a bit and leaned on me to keep his balance. "Haven't seen your pickup around Roderdale lately," he commented.

That's what I hated about Podunk towns like Roderdale and McClellan—everyone knew every-thing about everyone.

"Yeah, it's been a while."

Vox looked skeptically at me with one eye winked, but another swig drowned out his curiosity. While he drank, I looked around the party. I realized I recognized everyone but four people. Two of them were at least fifteen years older than me. Another one was dancing clumsily with Anika. The last one was leaning against the silver pickup, looking around exactly like I was.

I motioned Vox to bring his face closer to mine. "Who is that?" I whispered.

"That's Damon Vaughn. He's friends with Rhett. I think he's from Puter... 'Bout fifteen miles north of here."

Mentally, I figured up how far of a drive that would be from McClellan. Maybe forty-five minutes.

"Why?" Vox asked.

I gave him an honest answer. "He's cute."

"Well." Vox removed his arm from where it rested on my shoulders. "I'm gonna go get another beer."

Anika was still dancing with that guy, and it didn't look like she was going to be back anytime soon. I glanced at Damon again, trying not to be too obvious. One of the older guys had moved to stand next to him, but they weren't talking much, so I decided to make my move.

I wanted to chicken out a million and one times on my way over to him, but I forced one foot in front of the other. I didn't want to spend my summer pining over lost relationships when I had a cute guy standing feet from me.

Finally, I came to stand in front of him. "Hey," I said.

The old guy next to him reached an arm out and hooked a finger on my belt, pulling me closer.

"Hey, baby girl." His breath reeked of alcohol and chew.

"Get off me," I ordered, squirming away from him.

Damon reached out and pulled the guy's hands off me. "Leave her alone."

Damon's voice wasn't mean, but strong and steady, and I liked the smooth way it poured over his lips.

Apparently, the guy didn't want to mess with Damon. He dragged his feet as he stumbled off, mumbling something about "wasn't that hot anyways."

I leaned back against the pickup beside Damon, staring at the starry sky and trying to calm my nerves.

"Are you okay?" he asked.

Once I assured him that I was, he took a swig from his beer. Even though I didn't really drink, I admired the coordination it took to deter a major disaster without spilling a drop. Then, I admired everything else about him up close.

Damon was tall and thin with arms muscled from hard work, and from his tanned skin and scuffed boots, I guessed he'd spent a lot of time on a farm of some sort. The crown of my head came right under his chin, and the way he smiled at me with a set dreamy green eyes made me feel safe and excited and exposed in a way I'd never been before.

"So what's your name?" he asked.

"Skye."

He set his beer down on the pickup railing, held his hat to his chest, and stuck out his free hand to shake mine. It was rough and calloused and almost completely surrounded mine. "Damon Vaughn."

Kyle walked over to Damon and me and smiled at me. "How've you been, Skye?"

"Great," I said, a bit surprised. "How are you?"

I'd never known Kyle very well, but I'd talked to him after a few games freshman year, and we'd sat at the same table at prom when James and I went together.

"Good, good. You meet Damon yet?" he asked, gesturing toward Damon.

"Yeah, we just met," Damon said.

Kyle dipped his head toward me. "This is a good one."

Damon smirked. "Sure she's not trouble?"

Kyle aimed a flirty grin at me. "Might be, but isn't that half the fun?"

I smacked his arm. "I am not trouble!"

Kyle grinned, unfazed. "It's a good thing."

Across the shop, Anika called Kyle, and he gave

me a nod before walking off. I sent a thankful smile her way. What was it about guys? None of them ever paid any attention to me, and then the moment one seemed even slightly interested, they flocked to me like buzzards on roadkill. Okay, maybe comparing myself to roadkill wasn't right, but still.

Damon pulled his phone out of his pocket and typed in his passcode.

Great. He was probably texting his girlfriend or something.

I turned to find Anika and spare myself rejection.

"Wait," Damon said. "Can I have your number?"

My negative mood flipped a 180. Of course you can have my number, cute cowboy!

Shoveling sand on my excitement, I shrugged and said, "Yeah, sure."

Damon handed the phone to me. "Wanna put it in?"

"Sure," I said again, taking it from him. Trying to keep my fingers from shaking, I typed in my name on the cracked screen and the digits to my cell phone number. I hit save and handed the phone back to him.

I plucked up my courage. "Text me."

He was about to say something when Rhett and Vox came over.

Rhett handed me a beer. "So, what's Skye been up to?"

"Nothing too much," I told him. "Where are you going to college next year?"

"A tech school in Austin. Diesel mechanics. You'll have to come down and party."

"Yeah?" My cheeks felt warm at his suggestive smile. "Sure." Fat chance my parents would ever let me. But no one here needed to know that.

Rhett and Vox talked to Damon and me for a while. I opened my beer and took a few sips, just so I wouldn't look awkward, but I didn't want to have more than that. It tasted horrible, and I still had to drive back to Anika's house.

Damon joined in the conversation every now and then, but mostly he was quiet, listening and laughing.

"Well, excuse me, I gotta go take a leak," Rhett said, and Vox took his spot beside me.

"So when are we gonna hang out then?" he asked.

I could have kicked him! Vox and I hardly knew each other, but Damon probably didn't know that.

What if he thought I was some player and wouldn't text me?

"Sometime when I'm not busy," I hedged.

I glanced at Damon to see what he thought, and he gave me a small smile under the brim of his hat. I returned it.

Anika finally came over to me with her friend and introduced him to me as a harvester named Jesse.

A new country song spilled over the speakers, and Anika looked wildly from me to her guy. "We have to dance."

He nodded dopily at her. "I'm game."

She gripped my forearm. "You too." She pointed at Damon. "And you."

Jesse led her to an empty space on the driveway, and I gave Damon a pained look. "You don't have to dance with me."

But he was already setting his drink down and taking my hand. "Why wouldn't I?"

My stomach took a tumble at his words and the way his calloused hand squeezed mine. I fell into step with him, matching my movements to the song. As the sound of wind and crickets and rustling leaves and warbling country music blended, I could finally see myself looking up. Not just because Damon was a full head taller than me and grinning in the most adorable way, but because this, my life, was looking up.

"What are you thinking?" he asked.

I adjusted my hand on his shoulder. "I'll tell if you do."

He chuckled low and bent his head down. "Is that so?"

I nodded.

His eyes met mine. "I think you're cute."

No matter how hard I tried, I couldn't help the giddy smile spreading across my face. I mimicked his voice. "Is that so?"

Another laugh. I could get used to that sound.

The wind blew a piece of hair in my face, and he brushed it back, the rough skin of his hands trailing over my cheek. Something about the way he did it—slow, sensual—sent lightning bolts to my core.

"What do you think about me?" he asked.

"I—"

"Skye," Anika said, "We gotta get back to the house."

Damon's hands fell from my hand and side, and I suddenly felt like something was missing.

Anika looked at her phone screen. "I'm sorry, but it's already 11:45."

I looked to Damon, not sure what to say.

"See you later," he said. "Soon."

Anika and I jogged to the Suburban and got in. She told me how to take dirt roads to her house so we wouldn't run into any cops. She'd been drinking, and even though I definitely wasn't drunk, I didn't want an officer to catch us and hand over MIPs.

I listened while she rambled on about Jesse and how she never does anything like that, but all I could think about was that handsome cowboy and whether he would text me or not.

Fifteen minutes later, I got an answer to that question.

Damon: You should come back and hang out. Everyone's 2 drunk 2 be any fun.

CHAPTER FORTY

I GOT to the school an hour before graduation to clean out my locker. About half of the stuff in it was crap—old assignments, food wrappers, or notes—but when I finally got to the bottom of my locker, I saw the edge of a picture sticking out under the corner of a book.

I picked it up and saw Shelby in her volleyball uniform—her senior picture.

Every year, the seniors passed out photos of themselves with little notes on the back. The one Kellum gave me telling me to have a good senior year was lodged safely in my journal.

Shelby must have slid hers in my locker and it just fell to the bottom. Part of me wanted to rip it up and burn it, part of me was anxious to see what she had to say, and a tiny, tiny, tiny part of me hoped that she'd finally written me an apology.

At long last, I turned over the picture.

Skye,
 It's been great getting to know you this year.
 Have fun in volleyball next year.
 Enjoy every moment. It goes by so fast.
 Shelby

The second I finished reading it, I realized more than a tiny part of me had been expecting some sort of acknowledgement of what had happened between us —of what she'd put me through.

I stood against the wall opposite my locker for support and slid down to the floor. I had so many regrets, so many questions. A million should-haves flew through my mind, tormenting me with all the things I could have done to stand up to Shelby. But what hurt the most was that she acted like it never happened. How could a person single-handedly ruin someone's life and not have so much as a simple apology?

I hugged my knees to my chest and rested my forehead against them.

Maybe some people never apologized. I was finally starting to understand that Shelby's actions hadn't been about me. She had her own demons to deal with. What she'd done wasn't okay, would never be okay, but I didn't need her apology to move on.

I could move on, be myself, because I knew who I was, knew how to treat people, and knew that no matter what anyone threw at me, I could rise above and decide how I reacted. I could create my own future, just like Andrew said.

CHAPTER FORTY-ONE

WHEN I SAW Rachel in her cap and gown after the ceremony, it was hard to hold back tears. She was the senior I'd miss the most. I approached her in the receiving line, still not ready to tell her goodbye.

Her light brown hair hung straight, brushing the shoulders of her shiny black robe. When I came to stand in front of her, a grin spread across her face. She stretched her arms out for a hug, and I leaned into the embrace.

"I'm gonna miss you sooo much," she said.

"I'm not going to miss you," I talked over my trembling bottom lip. "Because we're going to hang out this summer."

"Definitely."

We broke apart, and she kept her hands on my

shoulders, holding me at arm's length. "You'll be in my shoes before you know it."

I hoped she was right.

And then it was someone else's turn to hug her, wish her luck.

I moved on to the next person in the line of graduates. I hugged Evan, and he made a fart noise. Kellum even extended his arms when I made it to him.

I melted into his chest. He smelled so good, and for a second, I let myself imagine that we'd shared more than a date, that we'd gone to prom together and become something more. But it was a fantasy, and I knew that's where it belonged.

"Have fun next year," he said in my ear before he let go. "I'm going to miss you."

I didn't think on what that meant or if there was some deeper meaning. Instead, I left the school, thinking about graduations and moving on. Next year, I would be moving my tassel to the left side. I would wear one of those ridiculous gowns, and I would receive an ending to my high school life in the form of a diploma.

Would I be ready for that? Definitely.

CHAPTER 42

Saturday afternoon, Andrew asked for my number, and we texted for the first time in a long time. We weren't talking about anything special. Just places that would be fun to visit when we got old enough to travel and see the world. But it felt nice to talk again.

While waiting for him to reply, I put the finishing touches on my makeup. I had on jeans that accentuated my new curves, and I was wearing a new pair of brown and pink cowboy boots. I'd need them for work with Rhett's family over the summer, but for now, they were the nicest shoes I had.

Andrew: Maybe someday we'll be able to take a trip together.

My breath caught in my chest. I couldn't let

myself think about that. Not when things were over. Not when I had a guy coming to my house to pick me up for a date.

I dabbed on some lip gloss before texting him back.

Me: Maybe. As friends.

I looked in the mirror and used hairspray to tame my flyaway hairs, then I checked the time. 6:45 P.M. and one new message.

Andrew: Who says it has to be just as friends? ;)

I swallowed, thankful texting could hide how much his words affected me.

Me: I think that was me. :)

Me: Getting ready to go on a date. Talk later?

Back to the moment at hand. I looked back at the mirror to check my appearance for any flaws. My blue eyes looked wide and inviting—I'd checked the internet for new makeup ideas—and the perfect amount of blush accentuated my cheekbones. "Kissable" was a good word to describe my lips...at least, I hoped so.

My phone vibrated, and I sat on the couch across from Mom to read the text.

Andrew: A date?

Me: Yeah.

"What time's he getting here?" Mom asked.

I didn't have much time left. "Seven."

Andrew: Is it serious?

Me: No.

Me: But it could be.

Dots flashed across the screen and then disappeared, but no message came. What had he been typing?

I heard a pickup pull into the driveway and got up to grab my purse off the counter.

"What?" Mom said. "He's not coming inside?"

"Maybe on the second date." I hoped it would be enough to keep him from seeing all of our mess.

She leaned back into the couch, folding her arms across her chest. "Fine by me."

I tucked my phone into my back pocket. Then I took a deep, calming breath. "See you later, Mom."

"See ya."

My phone vibrated, but I ignored it. I pulled open our front door to see Damon.

He was leaning against his diesel pickup parked along our yard, waiting for me. In his hand was a single yellow daisy. Things were finally looking up.

Thank you for reading *Becoming Skye*! To read Skye's happily ever after, check out Loving Skye today.

LOVING SKYE:
SNEAK PEEK

CHAPTER ONE

I COULDN'T COME up with something like this in a daydream. Seeing a guy this good-looking parked in my driveway, leaning back against his rumbling pickup, holding a wildflower for me? Unreal.

I stepped down the sidewalk toward him, readier than ever for our date. For this new beginning.

He pushed off his truck and walked to meet me halfway. "Hey, good-lookin'."

"Hey, Damon." I took in the clean skin of his jaw, the exciting way his green eyes danced. They didn't need the sun to catch any light. My face could have been replaced with a heart-eye emoji, and it probably wouldn't have looked any different. "So..."

He grinned and handed me the flower. "This is for you."

I held the thin stem between my fingers. "Should I bring it inside?"

"Nah, come on." He walked around to his side of the pickup, and I went to the passenger door. I knew most guys didn't open doors, but I still felt a little disappointed as I gazed up at the seat in the lifted truck. I had to hang on to the handle and lift my leg way up to pull myself into the cab. A little help might have been nice.

Once I got inside, though, I totally forgot any disappointment I'd been feeling. The cab smelled great—like leather and hay—and with Damon grinning over at me, I couldn't complain.

I set my flower on the dash and buckled up.

He pulled out of the driveway, steering with one hand on the wheel in that confident way only country kids did—like he'd been driving since before he knew how to do long division. "So, you ever been to a rodeo before?"

"Once," I admitted. "But I don't remember much."

"Okay, city slicker," he teased. "I'll getcha up to speed."

I made my eyes wide. "Promise?"

He bit his bottom lip and looked me up and down. "Definitely."

That look sent shockwaves right to my gut and flamed my cheeks. I gazed out my window. "Good."

He chuckled under his breath. "You're cute."

That had me staring back at him. "Yeah?"

A grin laced his full lips. "Uh huh."

My lips spread without asking my permission. "Thanks."

The houses flying by outside my window thinned, and we pulled up to an outdoor arena surrounded by vehicles and livestock trailers. As we drove into the grass parking lot, I watched people leading horses around, guys sitting on the fence talking, and people finding seats in metal stands.

Damon slowed the pickup and backed into an empty spot along the arena fence. "Front row seats."

He hopped out, and I followed him around the back of the pickup. He dropped the tailgate, then hopped up easily, and I hated to admit that I was looking at his backside for way too long. Whatever magic they sewed into Wranglers was working for him.

Gross. Did I just think that? My cheeks heated. What was going on with me? But really, those pants.

Damon set up a couple of camping chairs in the bed and scooted a cooler between them like a little table. "How's it look?"

I grinned at the setup. "Not bad."

He looked it over and hopped down from the pickup, landing lightly, even in his cowboy boots. "Let me help you up."

Considering the tailgate was at least three and a half feet off the ground, I felt thankful for his thoughtfulness. But... "I'm not sure you can lift me. I can get up there."

He rolled his eyes. "If I can take on a fifteen-hundred-pound horse, I think I can handle you." The muscles on his arms backed him up.

My stomach swooped at the thought. "Okay."

He looped his hands a couple feet off the ground, and I stepped into his makeshift stirrup with my good leg. I rested my hand on his shoulder—his shoulder that rippled powerfully under my touch—and he lifted me up so easily I might have been on an escalator.

I turned around on the tailgate and smiled down at him. "Thanks."

His phone dinged in his pocket, and he looked at the screen. "Hey, you mind if I go and say hi to Rhett and Vox real quick?"

Yes, I mind. "No, that's fine."

He grinned like I'd passed some sort of test. "You're the best. Be right back."

Damon walked toward the spot about fifty yards down the arena fence where a bunch of guys were sitting, and I couldn't help the sinking feeling that hit my stomach. Was I being clingy for wanting him to spend time with just me on our first date?

I shoved the thoughts aside and settled into one of the chairs. After making sure the bed was decently clean, I set my purse beside me. This really was a nice date—even though it was late May, it wasn't too terribly hot, and I could imagine a sunset out here would be beautiful. Plus, this whole camper chair and cooler setup was adorable.

I opened the cooler and saw it was full of ice and different drinks. I plucked up a blue Gatorade, took a sip, and stuck it in the chair's cupholder.

Now what?

Damon wasn't walking toward me yet, so I pulled out my phone and checked my messages.

I gasped at what Andrew sent me.

***

Continue reading *Loving Skye* today!

ALSO BY KELSIE STELTING

Curvy Girls Can't Dance

Curvy Girls Can't Date Soldiers

Curvy Girls Can't Date Princes

Curvy Girls Can't Date Rock Stars

The Pen Pal Romance Series

Dear Adam

Fabio Vs. the Friend Zone

Sincerely Cinderella

The Sweet Water High Series: A Multi-Author Collaboration

Road Trip with the Enemy: A Sweet Standalone Romance

YA Contemporary Romance Anthology

The Art of Taking Chances

Two More Days

Nonfiction

Raising the West

ACKNOWLEDGMENTS

Never in my imagination—which, as a writer, is pretty wild—did I think I'd be writing a continuous series. Because, frankly, it's hard! I have so many people to thank for getting me to "the end" on book two of Skye's story.

First, I need to thank everyone who helped me wrestle with *Becoming Skye*. My husband, Ty, who has read this story in many of its forms, my mom, who listened to me go on and on about it on multiple phone calls, and my writing friends, the YA Chicks, who plotted and outlined and commiserated over this story. *Becoming Skye* would be somewhere in the digital dumpster if it weren't for your help.

Many thanks to my editor, Yesenia Vargas, who helped make this story spick and span, and my critique partners, Cindy Ray Hale and Sally Henson, for helping me work through the plot.

I'd also like to thank my entire family, including my parents, husband, siblings, and grandparents for supporting me as a writer. I know they don't always understand why I spend so much time behind a glowing computer screen, tuning out everything going on around me, but they support my dreams nonetheless. I am incredibly fortunate to have so many great people in my corner.

To my advanced readers and reviewers, thank you for supporting me as a writer. Your feedback means so much to me, and I am beyond thankful you give your time to these stories.

And to you, the person holding this book. Thank you. From the bottom of my heart and soul, thank you. It's no secret that I think readers are some of the best people in the world, and I am in awe of you for letting your mind be whisked away into Skye's world, for giving your time to live someone else's story, and to read my words. I promise I work hard to make sure they're the very best they can be.

AUTHOR'S NOTE

I can't believe I'm here, writing the author's note for my eighth book. Writing a novel is challenging, and every time I finish one, it hits me as a surprise. I don't know why—I'm stubborn as heck and can do what I set my mind to. Plus, I've done it before. But mostly, it shouldn't come as a shock because all of the things I've been through have shown me how much I can accomplish if I don't give up.

In the story, Skye's endured many hard times. She lost who she thought were her best friends, she went through severe physical injury, her dreams of playing college volleyball were shattered, and her heart was completely broken. But she made it through. Even though she had to stand on an injured leg, she was still standing. And like she said, sometimes that has to be enough.

I wish I could tell you—tell myself—that you get through your hard times and things are easier, but that would be a dangerous lie. Life doesn't give us a promise, like, "Here's your crisis and now you're done." As my grandparents' Sunday school teacher likes to say, "God never promised us a smooth journey, only a safe landing."

So, if the journey's going to be rough, make yourself rougher. You have every single thing it takes inside of you to be a blessing to yourself and others. Love hard, fight for yourself and others, and never, ever stop chasing your dreams and cheering others on as they chase theirs. At the end of the day, dreams are what make crazy things like climbing mountains and building skyscrapers and even writing books possible. Never let that go.

Kelsie Stelting is a body positive romance author who writes love stories with strong characters, deep feelings, and happy endings.

She currently lives in Colorado. You can often find her writing, spending time with family, and soaking up too much sun wherever she can find it.

Visit www.kelsiestelting.com to get a free story and sign up for her readers' group!

Visit www.kelsiestelting.com to get a free story and sign up for her readers' group!

facebook.com/kelsiesteltingcreative

twitter.com/kelsiestelting

instagram.com/kelsiestelting

Made in United States
Troutdale, OR
05/08/2024

19755307R10202